DOVER · THRIFT · EDITIONS

All's Well
That Ends Well

WILLIAM SHAKESPEARE

DOVER PUBLICATIONS, INC.
Mineola, New York

DOVER THRIFT EDITIONS

GENERAL EDITOR: PAUL NEGRI
EDITOR OF THIS VOLUME: JOHN BERSETH

Copyright

Copyright © 2001 by Dover Publications, Inc.
All rights reserved.

Theatrical Rights

This Dover Thrift Edition may be used in its entirety, in adaptation, or in any other way for theatrical productions, professional and amateur, in the United States, without fee, permission, or acknowledgment. (This may not apply outside of the United States, as copyright conditions may vary.)

Bibliographical Note

This Dover edition, first published in 2001, contains the unabridged text of *All's Well That Ends Well* as published in Volume III of *The Caxton Edition of the Complete Works of William Shakespeare*, Caxton Publishing Company, London, n.d. The Note was prepared specially for this edition, and explanatory footnotes from the Caxton edition have been revised.

International Standard Book Number: 0-486-41593-7

Manufactured in the United States by Courier Corporation
41593702
www.doverpublications.com

Note

WILLIAM SHAKESPEARE (1564–1616) was born in Stratford-on-Avon, Warwickshire, England. Little is known with certainty about his early life. He moved to London c.1589 and began to make a living as both actor and playwright. Around 1594 he joined an acting company known as the Lord Chamberlain's Men. Immensely successful, he wrote thirty-seven plays, but only eighteen were published during his lifetime. These plays, sold directly to theater companies, were often printed in single-play editions without his approval. The earliest collected edition, known as the First Folio, was published in 1623. Since then, many other editions, with variant readings as well as outright errors, have been issued. But Shakespeare wrote plays specifically for performance, and his works drew popular audiences in his own day. Even today, almost 450 years after his birth, Shakespeare is still known around the world as a great dramatist and a gifted poet.

All's Well That Ends Well was most probably first performed in 1602-1603 but was not printed until the First Folio was issued. It was, according to the folklorist Andrew Lang and other scholars, titled *Love's Labors Won* in an earlier version. *All's Well* is one of Shakespeare's so-called dark comedies, in which he took a somewhat ill-tempered view of humanity. Good triumphs over evil in the end, but not before traveling a long and bumpy road. The play's story is based on the folktale of Giglietta di Nerbona (third day, ninth story) in Boccaccio's *Decameron*. It was translated by William Paynter, who included it in his *The Palace of Pleasure* (1566). But many of the characters are classically Shakespearean—the clowns, the garrulous old man, the benevolent ruler, the beautiful heroine, and the devious counselor, Paroles. Relatively unpopular with readers and audiences in the 18th and 19th centuries, *All's Well* has found favor in more recent times with people who appreciated its satiric, cynical, and morally ambivalent view of society.

Contents

Contents

Dramatis Personæ[1]

KING OF FRANCE.
DUKE OF FLORENCE.
BERTRAM, Count of Rousillon.
LAFEU, an old lord.
PAROLLES, a follower of Bertram.
Steward,
LAVACHE, a Clown, } servants to the Countess of Rousillon.
A Page.

COUNTESS OF ROUSILLON, mother to Bertram.
HELENA, a gentlewoman protected by the Countess.
An old Widow of Florence.
DIANA, daughter to the Widow.
VIOLENTA,
MARIANA, } neighbours and friends to the Widow.

Lords, Officers, Soldiers, &c., French and Florentine.

SCENE—*Rousillon; Paris; Florence; Marseilles*

---

[1]"All's Well" was printed for the first time in the Folio of 1623. There the text is divided into acts, but not into scenes, although the play opens with the words Actus Primus, Scæna Prima. Rowe first supplied scenic divisions, as well as a list of "dramatis personæ," in his edition of 1709.

ACT I.

SCENE I. *Rousillon: The Count's Palace.*

Enter BERTRAM, *the* COUNTESS OF ROUSILLON, HELENA, *and* LAFEU, *all in black*

COUNTESS. In delivering my son from me, I bury a second husband.

BER. And I in going, madam, weep o'er my father's death anew: but I must attend his majesty's command, to whom I am now in ward,[1] evermore in subjection.

LAF. You shall find of the king a husband, madam; you, sir, a father: he that so generally is at all times good, must of necessity hold his virtue to you; whose worthiness would stir it up where it wanted, rather than lack it where there is such abundance.[2]

COUNT. What hope is there of his majesty's amendment?

LAF. He hath abandoned his physicians, madam; under whose practices he hath persecuted time with hope,[3] and finds no other advantage in the process but only the losing of hope by time.

COUNT. This young gentlewoman had a father,—O, that "had"! how sad a passage 't is!—whose skill was almost as great as his honesty; had it stretched so far, would have made nature immortal, and death should have play for lack of work. Would, for the king's sake, he were living! I think it would be the death of the king's disease.

LAF. How called you the man you speak of, madam?

---

[1]*in ward*] In feudal and Elizabethan England heirs of great fortunes were invariably made wards of the king; he acted as their guardian.

[2]*he that so generally . . . abundance*] he that is so invariably kind must needs extend his (virtue of) kindness towards you, whose worth would be more likely to excite kindly feelings in those who are without them than to alienate them in one who is so richly endowed with them.

[3]*persecuted time with hope*] The general meaning is: Hope of recovery, fostered by his physicians, has hampered the action of (time in developing) the disease. But the only real effect (since the disease is not arrested) is to lose hope, as time goes on.

1

COUNT. He was famous, sir, in his profession, and it was his great
right to be so,—Gerard de Narbon.

LAF. He was excellent indeed, madam: the king very lately spoke of
him admiringly and mourningly: he was skilful enough to have
lived still, if knowledge could be set up against mortality.

BER. What is it, my good lord, the king languishes of?

LAF. A fistula, my lord.

BER. I heard not of it before.

LAF. I would it were not notorious. Was this gentlewoman the daughter of Gerard de Narbon?

COUNT. His sole child, my lord; and bequeathed to my overlooking.
I have those hopes of her good that her education promises; her
disposition she inherits, which makes fair gifts fairer; for where an
unclean mind carries virtuous qualities,[4] there commendations go
with pity;[5] they are virtues and traitors too: in her they are the better for their simpleness;[6] she derives her honesty and achieves her
goodness.

LAF. Your commendations, madam, get from her tears.

COUNT. 'T is the best brine a maiden can season her praise in. The
remembrance of her father never approaches her heart but the
tyranny of her sorrows takes all livelihood[7] from her cheek. No
more of this, Helena, go to, no more; lest it be rather thought you
affect a sorrow than to have—

HEL. I do affect a sorrow, indeed, but I have it too.

LAF. Moderate lamentation is the right of the dead; excessive grief
the enemy to the living.

COUNT. If the living be enemy to the grief, the excess makes it soon
mortal.[8]

BER. Madam, I desire your holy wishes.

LAF. How understand we that?

COUNT. Be thou blest, Bertram, and succeed thy father
In manners, as in shape! thy blood and virtue
Contend for empire in thee, and thy goodness
Share with thy birthright! Love all, trust a few,
Do wrong to none: be able for thine enemy
Rather in power than use; and keep thy friend
Under thy own life's key: be check'd for silence,

[4]*virtuous qualities*] qualities of good breeding, grace, erudition, the fruits of education:
not here qualities of moral virtue.
[5]*go with pity*] are to be regretted, are to be deprecated: *virtues and traitors*; excellences
which mislead as to the true character of their possessors.
[6]*simpleness*] singleness, integrity, freedom from deceit or uncleanness.
[7]*livelihood*] life, liveliness.
[8]*excess . . . mortal*] excessive indulgence in grief puts an end to it.

But never tax'd for speech. What heaven more will,
That thee may furnish, and my prayers pluck down,
Fall on thy head! Farewell, my lord;
'T is an unseason'd courtier; good my lord,
Advise him.

LAF.   He cannot want the best
That shall attend his love.

COUNT.   Heaven bless him! Farewell, Bertram.   [*Exit.*

BER. [*To* HELENA] The best wishes that can be forged in your
thoughts be servants to you! Be comfortable to my mother, your
mistress, and make much of her.

LAF.   Farewell, pretty lady: you must hold the credit of your father.

[*Exeunt* BERTRAM *and* LAFEU.

HEL.   O, were that all! I think not on my father;
And these great tears grace his remembrance more
Than those I shed for him.[9] What was he like?
I have forgot him: my imagination
Carries no favour in 't but Bertram's.
I am undone: there is no living, none,
If Bertram be away. 'T were all one
That I should love a bright particular star
And think to wed it, he is so above me:
In his bright radiance and collateral light
Must I be comforted, not in his sphere.
The ambition in my love thus plagues itself:
The hind that would be mated by the lion
Must die for love. 'T was pretty, though a plague,
To see him every hour; to sit and draw
His arched brows, his hawking eye, his curls,
In our heart's table; heart too capable
Of every line and trick of his sweet favour:
But now he's gone, and my idolatrous fancy
Must sanctify his reliques. Who comes here?

Enter PAROLLES

[*Aside*] One that goes with him: I love him for his sake;
And yet I know him a notorious liar.
Think him a great way fool, solely a coward;
Yet these fix'd evils sit so fit in him,
That they take place,[10] when virtue's steely bones

---

[9]*grace his remembrance . . . shed for him*] are mere ornamental tributes to his memory
rather than outpourings of past affection.
[10]*take place*] hold their own.

Look bleak i' the cold wind: withal, full oft we see
Cold wisdom waiting on superfluous folly.[11]

PAR.   Save you, fair queen!

HEL.   And you, monarch!

PAR.   No.

HEL.   And no.

PAR.   Are you meditating on virginity?

HEL.   Ay. You have some stain of soldier in you: let me ask you a question. Man is enemy to virginity; how may we barricado it against him?

PAR.   Keep him out.

HEL.   But he assails; and our virginity, though valiant, in the defence yet is weak: unfold to us some warlike resistance.

PAR.   There is none: man, sitting down before you, will undermine you and blow you up.

HEL.   Bless our poor virginity from underminers and blowers up! Is there no military policy, how virgins might blow up men?

PAR.   Virginity being blown down, man will quicklier be blown up: marry, in blowing him down again, with the breach yourselves made, you lose your city. It is not politic in the commonwealth of nature to preserve virginity. Loss of virginity is rational increase, and there was never virgin got till virginity was first lost. That you were made of is metal to make virgins. Virtinity by being once lost may be ten times found; by being ever kept, it is ever lost: 't is too cold a companion; away with 't!

HEL.   I will stand for 't a little, though therefore I die a virgin.

PAR.   There's little can be said in 't; 't is against the rule of nature. To speak on the part of virginity, is to accuse your mothers; which is most infallible disobedience. He that hangs himself is a virgin: virginity murders itself; and should be buried in highways out of all sanctified limit, as a desperate offendress against nature. Virginity breeds mites, much like a cheese; consumes itself to the very paring, and so dies with feeding his own stomach. Besides, virginity is peevish, proud, idle, made of self-love, which is the most inhibited sin in the canon. Keep it not; you cannot choose but lose by 't: out with 't! within ten years it will make itself ten,[12] which is a goodly increase; and the principle itself not much the worse: away with 't!

HEL.   How might one do, sir, to lose it to her own liking?

PAR.   Let me see: marry, ill, to like him that ne'er it likes. 'T is a

---

[11]*Cold wisdom . . . folly*] cheerless wisdom holding a place of inferiority to folly, which has no call to exist.

[12]*ten*] The First Folio reads *two. Ten,* which is Hanmer's emendation, is obviously correct.

commodity will lose the gloss with lying; the longer kept, the less worth: off with 't while 't is vendible; answer the time of request. Virginity, like an old courtier, wears her cap out of fashion; richly suited, but unsuitable: just like the brooch and the tooth-pick, which wear not now.[13] Your date[14] is better in your pie and your porridge than in your cheek: and your virginity, your old virginity, is like one of our French withered pears, it looks ill, it eats drily; marry, 't is a withered pear; it was formerly better; marry, yet 't is a withered pear: will you any thing with it?

HEL.   Not my virginity yet. . . .
There shall your master have a thousand loves,
A mother and a mistress and a friend,
A phœnix, captain, and an enemy,
A guide, a goddess, and a sovereign,
A counsellor, a traitress, and a dear;
His humble ambition, proud humility,
His jarring concord, and his discord dulcet,
His faith, his sweet disaster; with a world
Of pretty, fond, adoptious christendoms,
That blinking Cupid gossips.[15] Now shall he—
I know not what he shall. God send him well!
The court's a learning place, and he is one—

PAR.   What one, i' faith?
HEL.   That I wish well. 'T is pity—
PAR.   What's pity?
HEL.   That wishing well had not a body in 't,
Which might be felt; that we, the poorer born,
Whose baser stars do shut us up in wishes,
Might with effects of them follow our friends,
And show what we alone must think, which never
Returns us thanks.

Enter PAGE

PAGE.   Monsieur Parolles, my lord calls for you.   [*Exit.*
PAR.   Little Helen, farewell: if I can remember thee,
I will think of thee at court.
HEL.   Monsieur Parolles, you were born under a charitable star.
PAR.   Under Mars, I.
HEL.   I especially think, under Mars.
PAR.   Why under Mars?

[13]*wear not now*] are now out of fashion.
[14]*date*] a pun on the word in its two senses of "fruit" and "time of life."
[15]*adoptious . . . gossips*] assumed Christian names, for which purblind Love is sponsor.

HEL.   The wars have so kept you under, that you must needs be born
       under Mars.
PAR.   When he was predominant.
HEL.   When he was retrograde, I think, rather.
PAR.   Why think you so?
HEL.   You go so much backward when you fight.
PAR.   That's for advantage.
HEL.   So is running away, when fear proposes the safety: but the com-
       position that your valour and fear makes in you is a virtue of a
       good wing,[16] and I like the wear well.
PAR.   I am so full of businesses, I cannot answer thee acutely. I will re-
       turn perfect courtier; in the which, my instruction shall serve to
       naturalize thee, so thou wilt be capable of a courtier's counsel,
       and understand what advice shall thrust upon thee; else thou diest
       in thine unthankfulness, and thine ignorance makes thee away:
       farewell. When thou hast leisure, say thy prayers; when thou hast
       none, remember thy friends: get thee a good husband, and use
       him as he uses thee: so, farewell.   [*Exit.*
HEL.   Our remedies oft in ourselves do lie,
       Which we ascribe to heaven: the fated sky
       Gives us free scope; only doth backward pull
       Our slow designs when we ourselves are dull.
       What power is it which mounts my love so high;
       That makes me see, and cannot feed mine eye?
       The mightiest space in fortune nature brings
       To join like likes and kiss like native things.
       Impossible be strange attempts to those
       That weigh their pains in sense, and do suppose
       What hath been cannot be:[17] who ever strove
       To show her merit, that did miss her love?
       The king's disease—my project may deceive me,
       But my intents are fix'd, and will not leave me.   [*Exit.*

---

[16]*composition . . . wing*] valour, which causes you to run (backward, as you say, to get
up impetus), and fear, which also impels you to run (away), make up your being, of
which the power of flight is consequently the main characteristic.

[17]*The mightiest space . . . cannot be*] The widest difference of fortune is bridged by nature, which brings together like objects, however far apart they may happen to be, and
makes things of inherent similitude kiss or unite, whatever distance separates them.
Impossible are unusual attempts to those who judge their efforts by normal experience
and suppose that an exceptional occurrence can never recur. Hanmer's generally ac-
cepted change of *What hath been* into *What hath not been* scarcely improves the
sense and injures the metre.

SCENE II. *Paris: The King's Palace.*

Flourish of cornets. Enter the KING OF FRANCE *with letters, and divers*
    Attendants

KING. The Florentines and Senoys[1] are by the ears;
    Have fought with equal fortune, and continue
    A braving war.
FIRST LORD. So 't is reported, sir.
KING. Nay, 't is most credible; we here receive it
    A certainty, vouch'd from our cousin Austria,
    With caution, that the Florentine will move us
    For speedy aid; wherein our dearest friend
    Prejudicates the business, and would seem
    To have us make denial.
FIRST LORD.   His love and wisdom,
    Approved so to your majesty, may plead
    For amplest credence.
KING.   He hath arm'd[2] our answer,
    And Florence is denied before he comes:
    Yet, for our gentlemen that mean to see
    The Tuscan service, freely have they leave
    To stand on either part.
SEC. LORD.   It well may serve
    A nursery to our gentry, who are sick
    For breathing and exploit.
KING.   What's he comes here?

Enter BERTRAM, LAFEU, *and* PAROLLES

FIRST LORD. It is the Count Rousillon, my good lord,
    Young Bertram.
KING.   Youth, thou bear'st thy father's face;
    Frank nature, rather curious than in haste,
    Hath well composed thee. Thy father's moral parts
    Mayst thou inherit too! Welcome to Paris.
BER. My thanks and duty are your majesty's.
KING. I would I had that corporal soundness now,
    As when thy father and myself in friendship
    First tried our soldiership! He did look far
    Into the service of the time, and was

---

[1]*Senoys*] This is Painter's rendering in *The Palace of Pleasure* of Boccaccio's "Sanesi,"
    i.e. the people of Sienna.
[2]*arm'd*] made ready, or confirmed.

Discipled of the bravest: he lasted long;
But on us both did haggish age steal on,
And wore us out of act. It much repairs me
To talk of your good father. In his youth
He had the wit, which I can well observe
To-day in our young lords; but they may jest
Till their own scorn return to them unnoted
Ere they can hide their levity in honour:
So like a courtier, contempt nor bitterness
Were in his pride or sharpness; if they were,
His equal had awaked them;[3] and his honour,
Clock to itself, knew the true minute when
Exception[4] bid him speak, and at this time
His tongue obey'd his hand: who were below him
He used as creatures of another place;[5]
And bow'd his eminent top to their low ranks,
Making them proud of his humility,
In their poor praise he[6] humbled. Such a man
Might be a copy to these younger times;
Which, follow'd well, would demonstrate them now
But goers backward.

BER.   His good remembrance, sir,
Lies richer in your thoughts than on his tomb;
So in approof lives not his epitaph
As in your royal speech.[7]

KING.   Would I were with him! He would always say—
Methinks I hear him now; his plausive words
He scatter'd not in ears, but grafted them,
To grow there and to bear,—"Let me not live,"—
This his good melancholy oft began,
On the catastrophe and heel of pastime,
When it was out,—"Let me not live," quoth he,

---

[3]*they may jest . . . awaked them*] they may go on jesting till they wear all point out of their gibes before they can cover their petty follies with meritorious achievement. He was so courtierlike, so urbane, that there was nothing of contempt in his dignified bearing nor aught of bitterness in his keenness of wit. If bitterness or scorn ever appeared, it was a man of his own rank who evoked them.

[4]*Exception*] Blame, disapproval, the duty to take exception.

[5]*creatures of another place*] of another and of superior rank to that which they really occupied.

[6]*In their poor praise he*] At their simple praises of him he showed signs of modesty or humility.

[7]*So in approof . . . royal speech*] His epitaph does not supply such confirmation of his merits as does the speech of the King.

"After my flame lacks oil, to be the snuff
Of younger spirits, whose apprehensive senses
All but new things disdain;[8] whose judgements are
Mere fathers of their garments; whose constancies
Expire before their fashions." This he wish'd:
I after him do after him wish too,
Since I nor wax nor honey can bring home,
I quickly were dissolved[9] from my hive,
To give some labourers room.

SEC. LORD.   You are loved, sir;
They that least lend it you shall lack you first.

KING.   I fill a place, I know 't. How long is 't count,
Since the physician at your father's died?
He was much famed.

BER.   Some six months since, my lord.

KING.   If he were living, I would try him yet.
Lend me an arm; the rest have worn me out
With several applications: nature and sickness
Debate it at their leisure. Welcome, count;
My son's no dearer.

BER.   Thank your majesty.   [*Exeunt. Flourish.*

SCENE III. *Rousillon: The Count's Palace.*

Enter COUNTESS, Steward, *and* Clown

COUNT.   I will now hear; what say you of this gentlewoman?

STEW.   Madam, the care I have had to even your content,[1] I wish
might be found in the calendar[2] of my past endeavours; for then
we wound our modesty and make foul the clearness of our de-
servings, when of ourselves we publish them.[3]

COUNT.   What does this knave here? Get you gone, sirrah: the com-
plaints I have heard of you I do not all believe: 't is my slowness
that I do not; for I know you lack not folly to commit them, and
have ability enough to make such knaveries yours.

CLO.   'T is not unknown to you, madam, I am a poor fellow.

---

[8]*the snuff . . . disdain*] used-up wick, useless cinders, in the sight of younger spirits,
whose alert minds disdain all but new things.
[9]*dissolved*] separated, cut off, discharged.

---

[1]*to even your content*] to do precisely what you wish.
[2]*calendar*] record.
[3]*make foul . . . publish them*] obscure the grounds of our deserts.

COUNT. Well, sir.

CLO. No, madam, 't is not so well that I am poor, though many of the rich are damned: but, if I may have your ladyship's good will to go to the world,[4] Isbel the woman and I will do as we may.

COUNT. Wilt thou needs be a beggar?

CLO. I do beg your good will in this case.

COUNT. In what case?

CLO. In Isbel's case and mine own. Service is no heritage:[5] and I think I shall never have the blessing of God till I have issue o' my body; for they say barnes are blessings.

COUNT. Tell me thy reason why thou wilt marry.

CLO. My poor body, madam, requires it: I am driven on by the flesh; and he must needs go that the devil drives.

COUNT. Is this all your worship's reason?

CLO. Faith, madam, I have other holy reasons, such as they are.

COUNT. May the world know them?

CLO. I have been, madam, a wicked creature, as you and all flesh and blood are; and, indeed, I do marry that I may repent.

COUNT. Thy marriage, sooner than thy wickedness.

CLO. I am out o' friends, madam; and I hope to have friends for my wife's sake.

COUNT. Such friends are thine enemies, knave.

CLO. You're shallow, madam, in great friends; for the knaves come to do that for me, which I am aweary of. He that ears my land spares my team, and gives me leave to in the crop; if I be his cuckold, he's my drudge: he that comforts my wife is the cherisher of my flesh and blood; he that cherishes my flesh and blood loves my flesh and blood; he that loves my flesh and blood is my friend: ergo, he that kisses my wife is my friend. If men could be contented to be what they are, there were no fear in marriage; for young Charbon the puritan and old Poysam[6] the papist, howsome'er their hearts are severed in religion, their heads are both one; they may joul horns together, like any deer i' the herd.

COUNT. Wilt thou ever be a foul-mouthed and calumnious knave?

CLO. A prophet I, madam; and I speak the truth the next way:

---

[4]*to go to the world*] to get married: a common phrase.

[5]*Service is no heritage*] A common proverb, with which the speaker associates a reminiscence, of *Ps.* cxxvii, 3: "Lo, children are an heritage of the Lord."

[6]*Charbon . . . Poysam*] It has been ingeniously conjectured that these names are formed from the French words "chair bonne" (*i.e.*, good flesh), and "poisson" (*i.e.*, fish), and that reference is made to the Lenten fare characteristic respectively of Puritan and Papist. There is an old French proverb, "Jeune chair et vieil poisson" (meaning that meat is best eaten when the animal is young, fish when old and fat), which may well have suggested the collocation of the words, with their epithets.

>   For I the ballad[7] will repeat,
>   Which men full true shall find;
>   Your marriage comes by destiny,
>   Your cuckoo sings by kind.

COUNT.   Get you gone, sir; I'll talk with you more anon.

STEW.   May it please you, madam, that he bid Helen come to you: of her I am to speak.

COUNT.   Sirrah, tell my gentlewoman I would speak with her; Helen I mean.

CLO.   Was this fair face the cause, quoth she,[8]
>   Why the Grecians sacked Troy?
>   Fond done, done fond,
>   Was this King Priam's joy?
>   With that she sighed as she stood,
>   With that she sighed as she stood,
>   And gave this sentence then;
>   Among nine bad if one be good,
>   Among nine bad if one be good,
>   There's yet one good in ten.

COUNT.   What, one good in ten? you corrupt the song, sirrah.

CLO.   One good woman in ten, madam; which is a purifying o' the song: would God would serve the world so all the year! we'd find no fault with the tithe-woman[9] if I were the parson: one in ten, quoth a'! an we might have a good woman born but one every blazing star, or at an earthquake, 't would mend the lottery well: a man may draw his heart out, ere a' pluck one.

COUNT.   You'll be gone, sir knave, and do as I command you.

CLO.   That man should be at woman's command, and yet no hurt done! Though honesty be no puritan, yet it will do no hurt; it will wear the surplice of humility over the black gown[10] of a big heart. I am going, forsooth: the business is for Helen to come hither.

>   [Exit.

COUNT.   Well, now.

STEW.   I know, madam, you love your gentlewoman entirely.

[7]*the ballad*] Cf. John Grange's *Golden Aphroditis*, 1577:
>   "As cuckoldes come by destinie,
>   So cuckowes sing by kind."

[8]*seq.*] An obvious quotation from some old ballad about the siege of Troy. Cf. "St. George and the Dragon," in Percy's *Reliques*, which opens:
>   "Of Hector's deeds did Homer sing; and of the sack of stately Troy,
>   What griefs fair Helena did bring, which was Sir Paris' only joy."

[9]*tithe-woman*] tenth woman. Probably the correct version of the song represented one woman to be bad out of every ten, a ratio which the clown roguishly reverses.

[10]*wear the surplice . . . black gown*] conform outwardly to the law. The reference is to the antipathy of the Puritan to the surplice which the law enjoined, and his exclusive devotion to the black gown.

COUNT. Faith, I do: her father bequeathed her to me; and she herself, without other advantage, may lawfully make title to as much love as she finds: there is more owing her than is paid; and more shall be paid her than she'll demand.

STEW. Madam, I was very late more near her than I think she wished me: alone she was, and did communicate to herself her own words to her own ears; she thought, I dare vow for her, they touched not any stranger sense. Her matter was, she loved your son: Fortune, she said, was no goddess, that had put such difference betwixt their two estates; Love no god, that would not extend his might, only where qualities were level; . . . queen of virgins,[11] that would suffer her poor knight surprised, without rescue in the first assault, or ransom afterward. This she delivered in the most bitter touch of sorrow that e'er I heard virgin exclaim in: which I held my duty speedily to acquaint you withal; sithence, in the loss that may happen, it concerns you something to know it.

COUNT. You have discharged this honesty; keep it to yourself: many likelihoods informed me of this before, which hung so tottering in the balance, that I could neither believe nor misdoubt. Pray you, leave me: stall this in your bosom; and I thank you for your honest care: I will speak with you further anon. [*Exit Steward.*

Enter HELENA

Even so it was with me when I was young:
If ever we are nature's, there are ours; this thorn
Doth to our rose of youth rightly belong;
Our blood to us, this to our blood is born;
It is the show and seal of nature's truth,
Where love's strong passion is impress'd in youth:
By our remembrances of days foregone,
Such were our faults, or then we thought them none.
Her eye is sick on 't: I observe her now.

HEL. What is your pleasure, madam?

COUNT. You know, Helen,
I am a mother to you.

HEL. Mine honourable mistress.

COUNT. Nay, a mother:
Why not a mother? When I said "a mother,"
Methought you saw a serpent: what's in "mother,"

---

[11]*queen of virgins*] The obvious lacuna in this line evoked Theobald's brilliant emendation, *Diana no queen of virgins*, which is commonly adopted. This reading, which should be compared with the second line on page 15 ("your Dian"), implies that "poor knight" is "a poor *female* votary."

That you start at it? I say, I am your mother;
And put you in the catalogue of those
That were enwombed mine: 't is often seen
Adoption strives with nature; and choice breeds
A native slip to us from foreign seeds:
You ne'er oppress'd me with a mother's groan,
Yet I express to you a mother's care:
God's mercy, maiden! does it curd thy blood
To say I am thy mother? What's the matter,
That this distemper'd messenger of wet,
The many-colour'd Iris, rounds thine eye?
Why? that you are my daughter?

HEL.   That I am not.

COUNT.   I say, I am your mother.

HEL.   Pardon, madam;
The Count Rousillon cannot be my brother:
I am from humble, he from honour'd name;
No note upon my parents, his all noble:
My master, my dear lord he is; and I
His servant live, and will his vassal die:
He must not be my brother.

COUNT.   Nor I your mother?

HEL.   You are my mother, madam; would you were,—
So that my lord your son were not my brother,—
Indeed my mother! or were you both our mothers,
I care no more for than I do for heaven,
So I were not his sister. Can't no other,
But I your daughter, he must be my brother?

COUNT.   Yes, Helen, you might be my daughter-in-law:
God shield you mean it not! daughter and mother
So strive upon your pulse.[12] What, pale again?
My fear hath catch'd your fondness: now I see
The mystery of your loneliness,[13] and find
Your salt tears' head: now to all sense 't is gross
You love my son; invention is ashamed,
Against the proclamation of thy passion,[14]
To say thou dost not: therefore tell me true;
But tell me then, 't is so; for, look, thy cheeks
Confess it, th' one to th' other; and thine eyes

---

[12]*So strive . . . pulse*] So strain, excite your feeling.
[13]*loneliness*] Theobald's admirable emendation for the old reading *loveliness*.
[14]*invention . . . passion*] Falsehood would be ashamed to deny the fact in face of the plain avowal you made of your passion.

See it so grossly shown in thy behaviours,
That in their kind they speak it: only sin
And hellish obstinacy tie thy tongue,
That truth should be suspected. Speak, is 't so?
If it be so, you have wound a goodly clew;
If it be not, forswear 't: howe'er, I charge thee,
As heaven shall work in me for thine avail,
To tell me truly.

HEL.   Good madam, pardon me!

COUNT. Do you love my son?

HEL.   Your pardon, noble mistress!

COUNT. Love you my son?

HEL.   Do not you love him, madam?

COUNT. Go not about; my love hath in 't a bond,
Whereof the world takes note: come, come, disclose
The state of your affection; for your passions
Have to the full appeach'd.[15]

HEL.   Then, I confess,
Here on my knee, before high heaven and you,
That before you, and next unto high heaven,
I love your son.
My friends were poor, but honest; so's my love:
Be not offended; for it hurts not him
That he is loved of me: I follow him not
By any token of presumptuous suit;
Nor would I have him till I do deserve him;
Yet never know how that desert should be.
I know I love in vain, strive against hope;
Yet, in this captious and intenible sieve,[16]
I still pour in the waters of my love,
And lack not to lose still: thus, Indian-like,
Religious in mine error, I adore
The sun, that looks upon his worshipper,
But knows of him no more. My dearest madam,
Let not your hate encounter with my love
For loving where you do: but if yourself,
Whose aged honour[17] cites a virtuous youth,

---

[15]*Have . . . appeach'd*] Have given accusatory evidence, have "peached," in the slang sense.

[16]*captious and intenible sieve*] Both words, in the senses which are required by the context, are not met with elsewhere. "Captious" seems equivalent to "capacious," capable of receiving large quantities; "intenible" is its antithesis, "incapable of retaining."

[17]*Whose aged honour*] Whose honourable conduct in age proves that you were virtuous in youth.

Did ever in so true a flame of liking
Wish chastely and love dearly, that your Dian
Was both herself and love;[18] O, then, give pity
To her, whose state is such, that cannot choose
But lend and give where she is sure to lose;
That seeks not to find that her search implies,
But riddle-like lives sweetly where she dies!

COUNT.   Had you not lately an intent,—speak truly,—
To go to Paris?

HEL.   Madam, I had.

COUNT.   Wherefore? tell true.

HEL.   I will tell truth; by grace itself I swear.
You know my father left me some prescriptions
Of rare and proved effects, such as his reading
And manifest experience had collected
For general sovereignty;[19] and that he will'd me
In heedfull't reservation to bestow them,
As notes, whose faculties inclusive were,
More than they were in note:[20] amongst the rest,
There is a remedy, approved, set down,
To cure the desperate languishings whereof
The king is render'd lost.

COUNT.   This was your motive
For Paris, was it? speak.

HEL.   My lord your son made me to think of this;
Else Paris, and the medicine, and the king,
Had from the conversation of my thoughts
Haply been absent then.

COUNT.   But think you, Helen,
If you should tender your supposed aid,
He would receive it? he and his physicians
Are of a mind; he, that they cannot help him,
They, that they cannot help: how shall they credit
A poor unlearned virgin, when the schools,
Embowell'd of their doctrine,[21] have left off
The danger to itself?

---

[18]*your Dian . . . love*] The general meaning is, "The flame of liking" burned so purely
in you that the goddess of Chastity (Dian), whom you worshipped, suffered no men-
ace from your passion; in your case Love and Chastity were at one.

[19]*For general sovereignty*] To serve as a sovereign remedy of universal application.

[20]*As notes . . . note*] As prescriptions, whose inherent efficacy was greater than it was reputed to be.

[21]*Embowell'd of their doctrine*] Exhausted of their learning.

HEL.   There's something in 't,
    More than my father's skill, which was the great'st
    Of his profession, that[22] his good receipt
    Shall for my legacy be sanctified
    By the luckiest stars in heaven: and, would your honour
    But give me leave to try success,[23] I 'ld venture
    The well-lost life of mine on his Grace's cure
    By such a day and hour.
COUNT. Dost thou believe 't?
HEL.   Ay, madam, knowingly.
COUNT.   Why, Helen, thou shalt have my leave and love,
    Means and attendants, and my loving greetings
    To those of mine in court: I'll stay at home
    And pray God's blessing into thy attempt:
    Be gone to-morrow; and be sure of this,
    What I can help thee to, thou shalt not miss.   [*Exeunt.*

---

[22]*There's something . . . profession, that*] For *in 't* Hanmer substitutes *hints;* but the
change, though widely adopted, is needless, if we understand "that" in the common
Elizabethan sense of "to the effect that."
[23]*success*] issue, result. "Succeeding" is similarly used, II, page 30.

ACT II.

SCENE I. *Paris: The King's Palace.*

Flourish of cornets. Enter the KING, *attended with divers young* Lords
taking leave for the Florentine war; BERTRAM, *and* PAROLLES

KING.   Farewell, young lords; these warlike principles
    Do not throw from you: and you, my lords,[1] farewell:
    Share the advice betwixt you; if both gain, all
    The gift doth stretch itself as 't is received,
    And is enough for both.
FIRST LORD.   'T is our hope, sir,
    After well-enter'd soldiers,[2] to return
    And find your Grace in health.
KING.   No, no, it cannot be; and yet my heart
    Will not confess he owes the malady
    That doth my life besiege. Farewell, young lords;
    Whether I live or die, be you the sons
    Of worthy Frenchmen: let higher Italy,[3]—
    Those bated that inherit but the fall
    Of the last monarchy,—see that you come

---

[1]*young lords . . . my lords*] This is the reading of the First Folio. Hanmer proposed to read *lord* in the singular in each case, but the plural is fully justified. The king appears to address himself to two parties of lords, of which one was to fight on the side of Florence, and the other on the side of Sienna. Already—cf. page 7—he had given his courtiers leave to "stand on either part" in the Italian strife.

    In the First Folio the First Lord is called "Lord G." and the Second Lord "Lord E." The same initials are repeated in the case of another pair of French lords, who figure in Act IV, Scene iii. The initials "G" and "E" seem to be those of the actors who filled the parts in early productions of the piece. Goughe, Gilburne, and Ecclestone are mentioned among "the names of the principall actors in all these playes" in a preliminary page of the First Folio.

[2]*After well-enter'd soldiers*] After (we have become) well initiated, well-trained soldiers.

[3]*let higher Italy . . . monarchy*] let upper Italy—let your humbled foemen who inherit merely the decadence of the ended (Roman) empire.

17

Not to woo honour, but to wed it; when
The bravest questant shrinks, find what you seek,
That fame may cry you loud: I say, farewell.
SEC. LORD.   Health, at your bidding, serve your majesty!
KING.   Those girls of Italy, take heed of them:
They say, our French lack language to deny,
If they demand: beware of being captives,
Before you serve.
BOTH.   Our hearts receive your warnings.
KING.   Farewell. Come hither to me.   [*Exit.*
FIRST LORD.   O my sweet lord, that you will stay behind us!
PAR.   'T is not his fault, the spark.
SEC. LORD.   O, 't is brave wars!
PAR.   Most admirable: I have seen those wars.
BER.   I am commanded here, and kept a coil with[4]
"Too young," and "the next year," and "'t is too early."
PAR.   An thy mind stand to 't, boy, steal away bravely.
BER.   I shall stay here the forehorse to a smock,[5]
Creaking my shoes on the plain masonry,
Till honour be bought up, and no sword[6] worn
But one to dance with! By heaven, I'll steal away.
FIRST LORD.   There's honour in the theft.
PAR.   Commit it, count.
SEC. LORD.   I am your accessary; and so, farewell.
BER.   I grow to you, and our parting is a tortured body.
FIRST LORD.   Farewell, captain.
SEC. LORD.   Sweet Monsieur Parolles!
PAR.   Noble heroes, my sword and yours are kin. Good sparks and lus-
trous, a word, good metals: you shall find in the regiment of the
Spinii one Captain Spurio, with his cicatrice, an emblem of war,
here on his sinister cheek; it was this very sword entrenched it: say
to him, I live; and observe his reports for me.
FIRST LORD.   We shall, noble captain.   [*Exeunt* Lords.
PAR.   Mars dote on you for his novices! what will ye do?
BER.   Stay: the king.

Re-enter KING

PAR.   [*Aside to* BER.] Use a more spacious ceremony to the noble
lords; you have restrained yourself within the list of too cold an

[4]*kept a coil with*] pestered with fussy objections to my going.
[5]*the forehorse to a smock*] the squire of petticoats. The forehorse was the leading horse
of a team, and was often pranked out in ribbons.
[6]*no sword*] Men wore short swords when they danced.

adieu: be more expressive to them: for they wear themselves in the
cap of the time, there do muster true gait, eat, speak, and move[7]
under the influence of the most received star; and though the
devil lead the measure, such are to be followed: after them, and
take a more dilated farewell.

BER.   And I will do so.

PAR.   Worthy fellows; and like to prove most sinewy sword-men.

[*Exeunt* BERTRAM *and* PAROLLES.

Enter LAFEU

LAF.   [*Kneeling*] Pardon, my lord, for me and for my tidings.

KING.   I'll fee[8] thee to stand up.

LAF.   Then here's a man stands, that has brought his pardon.
I would you had kneel'd, my lord, to ask me mercy;
And that at my bidding you could so stand up.

KING.   I would I had; so I had broke thy pate,
And ask'd thee mercy for 't.

LAF.   Good faith, across:[9] but, my good lord, 't is thus;
Will you be cured of your infirmity?

KING.   No.

LAF.   O, will you eat no grapes, my royal fox?
Yes, but you will my noble grapes, an if
My royal fox could reach them: I have seen a medicine
That's able to breathe life into a stone,
Quicken a rock, and make you dance canary
With spritely fire and motion; whose simple touch
Is powerful to araise King Pepin, nay,
To give great Charlemain[10] a pen in 's hand,
And write to her a love-line.

KING.   What "her" is this?

LAF.   Why, Doctor She: my lord, there's one arrived,
If you will see her: now, by my faith and honour,
If seriously I may convey my thoughts
In this my light deliverance, I have spoke
With one that, in her sex, her years, profession,

[7]*in the cap of the time, . . . move*] in the height of the fashion; in them is concentrated
authentic etiquette in regard to eating, speaking, and moving

[8]*fee*] Theobald's correction of the Folio reading *see*. The meaning is, "I 'ld reward thee
if I could stand up."

[9]*across*] Lafeu's meaning is that the king's retort is clumsy. To thrust a lance in a tilting
match "across" [the body of] an adversary instead of pushing the point towards him was
a sign of awkwardness.

[10]*great Charlemain*] There was a tradition that Charlemagne late in life made a vain
endeavour to learn to write.

Wisdom and constancy, hath amazed me more
Than I dare-blame my weakness:[11] will you see her,
For that is her demand, and know her business?
That done, laugh well at me.
KING.   Now, good Lafeu,
Bring in the admiration; that we with thee
May spend our wonder too, or take off thine
By wondering how thou took'st it.
LAF.   Nay, I'll fit you,
And not be all day neither.   [*Exit.*
KING.   Thus he his special nothing ever prologues.

Re-enter LAFEU, *with* HELENA

LAF.   Nay, come your ways.
KING.   This haste hath wings indeed.
LAF.   Nay, come your ways;
This is his majesty, say your mind to him:
A traitor you do look like; but such traitors
His majesty seldom fears: I am Cressid's uncle,[12]
That dare leave two together; fare you well.   [*Exit.*
KING.   Now, fair one, does your business follow us?
HEL.   Ay, my good lord.
Gerard de Narbon was my father;
In what he did profess, well found.
KING.   I knew him.
HEL.   The rather will I spare my praises towards him;
Knowing him is enough. On 's bed of death
Many receipts he gave me; chiefly one,
Which, as the dearest issue of his practice,
And of his old experience the only darling,
He bade me store up, as a triple eye,[13]
Safer than mine own two, more dear; I have so:
And, hearing your high majesty is touch'd
With that malignant cause, wherein the honour
Of my dear father's gift stands chief in power,
I come to tender it and my appliance,
With all bound humbleness.
KING.   We thank you, maiden;
But may not be so credulous of cure,

[11]*Than I dare blame my weakness*] Than I care to admit for fear of exposing myself to
the reproach of weakness.
[12]*Cressid's uncle*] Pandarus, a leading character in Shakespeare's *Troil, and Cress.*
[13]*triple eye*] a third eye.

When our most learned doctors leave us, and
The congregated college have concluded
That labouring art can never ransom nature
From her inaidible estate; I say we must not
So stain our judgement, or corrupt our hope,
To prostitute our past-cure malady
To empirics, or to dissever so
Our great self and our credit, to esteem
A senseless help, when help past sense we deem.[14]

HEL.   My duty, then, shall pay me for my pains:
I will no more enforce mine office on you;
Humbly entreating from your royal thoughts
A modest one, to bear me back again.

KING.   I cannot give thee less, to be call'd grateful:
Thou thought'st to help me; and such thanks I give
As one near death to those that wish him live:
But, what at full I know, thou know'st no part;
I knowing all my peril, thou no art.

HEL.   What I can do can do no hurt to try,
Since you set up your rest 'gainst remedy.
He that of greatest works is finisher,
Oft does them by the weakest minister:
So holy writ in babes hath judgement shown,
When judges have been babes; great floods have flown
From simple sources; and great seas have dried,
When miracles have by the greatest been denied
Oft expectation fails, and most oft there
Where most it promises; and oft it hits
Where hope is coldest, and despair most fits.[15]

KING.   I must not hear thee; fare thee well, kind maid;
Thy pains not used must by thyself be paid:
Proffers not took reap thanks for their reward.

HEL.   Inspired merit so by breath is barr'd:
It is not so with Him that all things knows,
As 't is with us that square our guess by shows;
But most it is presumption in us when
The help of heaven we count the act of men.
Dear sir, to my endeavours give consent;
Of heaven, not me, make an experiment.

---

[14]*dissever so . . . deem*] I must not so disjoin my person and place from their fit dignity
by setting value on an ignorant offer of help, when I deem my case to be beyond the
reach of intelligent assistance.

[15]*fits*] Theobald's emendation for the Folio reading *shifts*.

I am not an impostor, that proclaim
Myself against the level of mine aim;[16]
But know I think, and think I know most sure,
My art is not past power, nor you past cure.

KING.   Art thou so confident? within what space
Hopest thou my cure?

HEL.   The great'st grace lending grace,
Ere twice the horses of the sun shall bring
Their fiery torcher his diurnal ring;[17]
Ere twice in murk and occidental damp
Moist Hesperus hath quench'd his sleepy lamp;
Or four and twenty times the pilot's glass
Hath told the thievish minutes how they pass;
What is infirm from your sound parts shall fly,
Health shall live free, and sickness freely die.

KING.   Upon thy certainty and confidence
What darest thou venture?

HEL.   Tax of impudence,
A strumpet's boldness, a divulged shame
Traduced by odious ballads: my maiden's name
Sear'd otherwise, ne worse of worst extended,[18]
With vilest torture let my life be ended.

KING.   Methinks in thee some blessed spirit doth speak
His powerful sound within an organ weak:
And what impossibility would slay
In common sense, sense saves another way.[19]
Thy life is dear; for all, that life can rate
Worth name of life, in thee hath estimate,
Youth, beauty, wisdom, courage,[20] all
That happiness and prime can happy call:
Thou this to hazard needs must intimate
Skill infinite or monstrous desperate.

---

[16]*proclaim . . . aim*] make professions which are not in accord with my real intentions.
"Level" is not uncommon in the sense of "purpose."

[17]*bring . . . ring*] carry their fiery torchbearer round his daily circuit or orbit.

[18]*ne worse of worst extended*] This is the reading of the First Folio. In the Second and
later folios *no* was substituted for *ne*. "Ne" usually means "nor," but the meaning
seems here to be "nay." Helena says: "let the worse come to the worst, let untoward
fate be strained to the worse degree of what is very bad, — in effect, let me die under
vilest torture."

[19]*And what impossibility . . . another way*] A notion, which, in virtue of its incredibility,
is liable to be destroyed by common sense, may survive after all; perception or sensa-
tion has means of preserving a notion in spite of its being rejected by ordinary reason.

[20]Theobald proposed to insert *virtue* after *courage*, so as to complete the metre.

Sweet practiser, thy physic I will try,
That ministers thine own death if I die.

HEL.   If I break time, or flinch in property[21]
Of what I spoke, unpitied let me die,
And well deserved: not helping, death's my fee;
But, if I help, what do you promise me?

KING.   Make thy demand.

HEL.   But will you make it even?[22]

KING.   Ay, by my sceptre and my hopes of heaven.

HEL.   Then shalt thou give me with thy kingly hand
What husband in thy power I will command:
Exempted be from me the arrogance
To choose from forth the royal blood of France,
My low and humble name to propagate
With any branch or image of thy state;
But such a one, thy vassal, whom I know
Is free for me to ask, thee to bestow

KING.   Here is my hand; the premises observed,
Thy will by my performance shall be served:
So make the choice of thy own time; for I,
Thy resolved patient, on thee still rely.
More should I question thee, and more I must,
Though more to know could not be more to trust,
From whence thou camest, how tended on: but rest
Unquestion'd welcome, and undoubted blest.
Give me some help here, ho! If thou proceed
As high as word, my deed shall match thy deed.

                                        [*Flourish. Exeunt.*

SCENE II. *Rousillon: The Count's Palace.*

Enter the COUNTESS *and* Clown

COUNT.   Come on, sir; I shall now put you to the height of your
        breeding.

CLO.   I will show myself highly fed and lowly taught: I know my busi-
        ness is but to the court.

COUNT.   To the court! why, what place make you special, when you
        put off that with such contempt? But to the court!

CLO.   Truly, madam, if God have lent a man any manners, he may

---

[21]*flinch in property*] fail in any essential particular.
[22]*make it even*] give precisely what is asked.

easily put it off at court: he that cannot make a leg, put off's cap,
kiss his hand, and say nothing, has neither leg, hands, lip, nor cap;
and, indeed, such a fellow, to say precisely, were not for the court;
but for me, I have an answer will serve all men.

COUNT.   Marry, that's a bountiful answer that fits all questions.

CLO.   It is like a barber's chair, that fits all buttocks, the pin-buttock,
the quatch-buttock, the brawn-buttock, or any buttock.

COUNT.   Will your answer serve fit to all questions?

CLO.   As fit as ten groats is for the hand of an attorney, as your French
crown for your taffeta punk, as Tib's rush[1] for Tom's forefinger, as
a pancake for Shrove Tuesday, a morris for May-day, as the nail to
his hole, the cuckold to his horn, as a scolding quean to a wran-
gling knave, as the nun's lip to the friar's mouth, nay, as the pud-
ding to his skin.

COUNT.   Have you, I say, an answer of such fitness for all questions?

CLO.   From below your duke to beneath your constable, it will fit any
question.

COUNT.   It must be an answer of most monstrous size that must fit all
demands.

CLO.   But a trifle neither, in good faith, if the learned should speak
truth of it: here it is, and all that belongs to 't. Ask me if I am a
courtier: it shall do you no harm to learn.

COUNT.   To be young again, if we could: I will be a fool in question,
hoping to be the wiser by your answer. I pray you, sir, are you a
courtier?

CLO.   O Lord, sir! There's a simple putting off. More, more, a hundred of them.

COUNT.   Sir, I am a poor friend of yours, that loves you.

CLO.   O Lord, sir! Thick, thick, spare not me.

COUNT.   I think, sir, you can eat none of this homely meat.

CLO.   O Lord, sir! Nay, put me to 't, I warrant you.

COUNT.   You were lately whipped, sir, as I think.

CLO.   O Lord, sir! spare not me.

COUNT.   Do you cry, "O Lord, sir!" at your whipping, and "spare not
me"? Indeed your "O Lord, sir!" is very sequent to your whipping:
you would answer very well to a whipping, if you were but bound
to 't.

CLO.   I ne'er had worse luck in my life in my "O Lord, sir!" I see
things may serve long, but not serve ever.

---

[1]*Tib's rush, etc.*] "Tib" and "Tom" were used for "lad" and "lass" much like "Jack" and
"Jill." "Tib's rush" means a ring made of a rush, commonly used in rural districts as a
love token.

COUNT. I play the noble housewife with the time,
　　　To entertain 't so merrily with a fool.
CLO. O Lord, sir! why, there 't serves well again.
COUNT. An end, sir; to your business. Give Helen this,
　　　And urge her to a present answer back:
　　　Commend me to my kinsmen and my son:
　　　This is not much.
CLO. Not much commendation to them.
COUNT. Not much employment for you: you understand me?
CLO. Most fruitfully: I am there before my legs.
COUNT. Haste you again.   [*Exeunt severally.*

SCENE III. *Paris: The King's Palace.*

Enter BERTRAM, LAFEU, *and* PAROLLES

LAF. They say miracles are past; and we have our philosophical per-
　　　sons, to make modern and familiar, things supernatural and cause-
　　　less.[1] Hence is it that we make trifles of terrors; ensconcing
　　　ourselves into seeming knowledge, when we should submit our-
　　　selves to an unknown fear.
PAR. Why, 't is the rarest argument of wonder that hath shot out in
　　　our latter times.
BER. And so 't is.
LAF. To be relinquished of the artists,—
PAR. So I say; both of Galen and Paracelsus.
LAF. Of all the learned and authentic fellows,—
PAR. Right; so I say.
LAF. That gave him out incurable,—
PAR. Why, there 't is; so say I too.
LAF. Not to be helped,—
PAR. Right; as 't were, a man assured of a—
LAF. Uncertain life, and sure death.
PAR. Just, you say well; so would I have said.
LAF. I may truly say, it is a novelty to the world.
PAR. It is, indeed: if you will have it in showing, you shall read it in—
　　　what do ye call there?
LAF. A showing of a heavenly effect in an earthly actor.
PAR. That 's it; I would have said the very same.

---

[1]*causeless*] Coleridge points out that a cause is only predicable of things natural (phe-
nomena), and that Shakespeare is strictly accurate from a philosophical point of view
in describing things supernatural (noumena) as "causeless," *i.e.* without mundane ori-
gin or connection with matter.

LAF.   Why, your dolphin is not lustier; 'fore me, I speak in respect—

PAR.   Nay, 't is strange, 't is very strange, that is the brief and the tedious of it; and he's of a most facinerious spirit that will not acknowledge it to be the—

LAF.   Very hand of heaven.

PAR.   Ay, so I say.

LAF.   In a most weak—

PAR.   And debile minister, great power, great transcendence: which should, indeed, give us a further use to be made than alone the recovery of the king, as to be—

LAF.   Generally thankful.

PAR.   I would have said it; you say well. Here comes the king.

Enter KING, HELENA, *and* Attendants

LAF.   Lustig,[2] as the Dutchman says: I'll like a maid the better, whilst I have a tooth in my head: why, he's able to lead her a coranto.

PAR.   Mort du vinaigre! is not this Helen?

LAF.   'Fore God, I think so.

KING.   Go, call before me all the lords in court.
Sit, my preserver, by thy patient's side;
And with this healthful hand, whose banish'd sense
Thou hast repeal'd, a second time receive
The confirmation of my promised gift,
Which but attends thy naming.

Enter three or four Lords

Fair maid, send forth thine eye: this youthful parcel
Of noble bachelors stand at my bestowing,
O'er whom both sovereign power and father's voice[3]
I have to use: thy frank election make;
Thou hast power to choose, and they none to forsake.

HEL.   To each of you one fair and virtuous mistress
Fall, when Love please! marry, to each, but one!

LAF.   I 'ld give bay Curtal and his furniture,
My mouth no more were broken than these boys',
And writ as little beard.

KING.   Peruse them well:
Not one of those but had a noble father.

HEL.   Gentlemen,
Heaven hath through me restored the king to health.

ALL.   We understand it, and thank heaven for you.

---

[2]*Lustig*] The Dutch word is "Lustigh," meaning lusty, vigorous.
[3]*father's voice*] father's approval.

HEL.   I am a simple maid; and therein wealthiest,
         That I protest I simply am a maid.
         Please it your majesty, I have done already:
         The blushes in my cheeks thus whisper me,
         "We blush that thou shouldst choose; but, be refused,
         Let the white death sit on thy cheek for ever;
         We'll ne'er come there again."

KING.   Make choice; and, see,
         Who shuns thy love shuns all his love in me.

HEL.   Now, Dian, from thy altar do I fly;
         And to imperial Love, that god most high,
         Do my sighs stream. Sir, will you hear my suit?

FIRST LORD.   And grant it.

HEL.   Thanks, sir; all the rest is mute.[4]

LAF.   I had rather be in this choice than throw ames-ace[5] for my life.

HEL.   The honour, sir, that flames in your fair eyes,
         Before I speak, too threateningly replies:
         Love make your fortunes twenty times above
         Her that so wishes and her humble love!

SEC. LORD.   No better, if you please.

HEL.   My wish receive,
         Which great Love grant! and so, I take my leave.

LAF.   Do all they deny her? An they were sons of mine, I 'ld have them
         whipped; or I would send them to the Turk, to make eunuchs of.

HEL.   Be not afraid that I your hand should take;
         I'll never do you wrong for your own sake:
         Blessing upon your vows! and in your bed
         Find fairer fortune, if you ever wed!

LAF.   These boys are boys of ice, they'll none have her: sure, they are
         bastards to the English; the French ne'er got 'em.

HEL.   You are too young, too happy, and too good,
         To make yourself a son out of my blood.

FOURTH LORD.   Fair one, I think not so.

LAF.   There's one grape yet; I am sure thy father drunk wine: but if
         thou be'st not an ass, I am a youth of fourteen; I have known thee
         already.[6]

HEL. [To BERTRAM]   I dare not say I take you; but I give

---

[4]*all the rest is mute*] I will say no more.
[5]*ames-ace*] ambs-ace, the two aces, the lowest throw of the dice, a thing of no value. The
   general meaning of Lafeu's somewhat lame irony seems to be, "I had rather be a com-
   petitor in this contest than risk my life for nothing at all."
[6]*I am sure . . . already*] Thy father put some spirit into you; but I know enough of you
   to know you for an ass.

Me and my service, ever whilst I live,
Into your guiding power. This is the man.

KING.   Why, then, young Bertram, take her; she's thy wife.

BER.   My wife, my liege! I shall beseech your highness,
In such a business give me leave to use
The help of mine own eyes.

KING.   Know'st thou not, Bertram,
What she has done for me?

BER.   Yes, my good lord;
But never hope to know why I should marry her.

KING.   Thou know'st she has raised me from my sickly bed.

BER.   But follows it, my lord, to bring me down
Must answer for your raising? I know her well:
She had her breeding at my father's charge.
A poor physician's daughter my wife! Disdain
Rather corrupt me ever![7]

KING.   'T is only title thou disdain'st in her, the which
I can build up. Strange is it, that our bloods,
Of colour,[8] weight, and heat, pour'd all together,
Would quite confound distinction, yet stand off
In differences so mighty. If she be
All that is virtuous, save what thou dislikest,
A poor physician's daughter, thou dislikest
Of virtue for the name: but do not so:
From lowest place when virtuous things proceed
The place is dignified by the doer's deed:
Where great additions swell's and virtue none,
It is a dropsied honour. Good alone
Is good without a name. Vileness is so:[9]
The property by what it is should go,
Not by the title. She is young, wise, fair;
In these to nature she's immediate heir,
And these breed honour: that is honour's scorn,
Which challenges itself as[10] honour's born,
And is not like the sire: honours thrive,
When rather from our acts we them derive
Than our foregoers: the mere word's a slave
Debosh'd on every tomb, on every grave
A lying trophy; and as oft is dumb

---

[7]*Disdain . . . ever*] May ignominy or disgrace otherwise taint me for ever.
[8]*Of colour, etc.*] As far as colour, etc., are concerned.
[9]*Vileness is so*] Vileness is in the same case.
[10]*challenges itself as*] asserts a claim to be.

Where dust and damn'd oblivion is the tomb
Of honour'd bones indeed. What should be said?
If thou canst like this creature as a maid,
I can create the rest: virtue and she
Is her own dower; honour and wealth from me.

BER.   I cannot love her, nor will strive to do 't.

KING.   Thou wrong'st thyself, if thou shouldst strive to choose.

HEL.   That you are well restored, my lord, I'm glad:
Let the rest go.

KING.   My honour's at the stake; which to defeat,[11]
I must produce my power. Here, take her hand,
Proud scornful boy, unworthy this good gift;
That dost in vile misprision shackle up[12]
My love and her desert; that canst not dream,
We, poising us in her defective scale,
Shall weigh thee to the beam;[13] that wilt not know,
It is in us to plant thine honour where
We please to have it grow. Check thy contempt:
Obey our will, which travails in thy good:
Believe not thy disdain, but presently
Do thine own fortunes that obedient right
Which both thy duty owes and our power claims;
Or I will throw thee from my care for ever
Into the staggers[14] and the careless lapse
Of youth and ignorance; both my revenge and hate
Loosing upon thee, in the name of justice,
Without all terms of pity. Speak; thine answer.

BER.   Pardon, my gracious lord; for I submit
My fancy to your eyes: when I consider
What great creation and what dole of honour
Flies where you bid it, I find that she, which late
Was in my nobler thoughts most base, is now
The praised of the king; who, so ennobled,
Is as 't were born so.

KING.   Take her by the hand,
And tell her she is thine: to whom I promise

---

[11]*which to defeat*] and to destroy this risk of injury to my honour.
[12]*in vile misprision shackle up*] contemptibly undervalue or disdain. "Misprision"
means here "the act of undervaluing."
[13]*We, poising . . . beam*] We, throwing the weight of our influence in her favour or scale,
which of itself were deficient in weight, shall make the scale in which you are placed
strike the beam, *i.e.*, weigh nothing at all.
[14]*staggers*] strictly speaking, apoplexy in horses. Here "staggering helplessness" or "be-
wilderment" (of men).

A counterpoise; if not to thy estate,
A balance more replete.
BER.   I take her hand.
KING.   Good fortune and the favour of the king
Smile upon this contract; whose ceremony
Shall seem expedient on the now-born brief,[15]
And be perform'd to-night: the solemn feast
Shall more attend upon the coming space,
Expecting absent friends.[16] As thou lovest her,
Thy love's to me religious; else, does err.

                          [*Exeunt all but* LAFEU *and* PAROLLES.

LAF.   Do you hear, monsieur? a word with you.
PAR.   Your pleasure, sir?
LAF.   Your lord and master did well to make his recantation.
PAR.   Recantation! My lord! my master!
LAF.   Ay; is it not a language I speak?
PAR.   A most harsh one, and not to be understood without bloody suc-
ceeding.[17] My master!
LAF.   Are you companion to the Count Rousillon?
PAR.   To any count, to all counts, to what is man.
LAF.   To what is count's man: count's master is of another style.
PAR.   You are too old, sir; let it satisfy you, you are too old.
LAF.   I must tell thee, sirrah, I write man;[18] to which title age cannot
bring thee.
PAR.   What I dare too well do, I dare not do.
LAF.   I did think thee, for two ordinaries,[19] to be a pretty wise fellow;
thou didst make tolerable vent of thy travel; it might pass: yet the
scarfs and the bannerets about thee did manifoldly dissuade me
from believing thee a vessel of too great a burthen. I have now
found thee; when I lose thee again, I care not: yet art thou good
for nothing but taking up;[20] and that thou 'rt scarce worth.
PAR.   Hadst thou not the privilege of antiquity upon thee,—
LAF.   Do not plunge thyself too far in anger, lest thou hasten thy trial;

---

[15]*Shall seem expedient on the now-born brief*] Shall rightly follow immediately on the
short and summary engagement. "Brief" here means "a short" verbal assurance. Cf.
note 17, page 80, "a sweet verbal *brief.*"
[16]*Shall more attend . . . friends*] shall take place at a longer interval hereafter, awaiting
the coming of absent friends.
[17]*succeeding*] sequel, result, issue. "Success" is similarly used. See note 23, page 16.
[18]*I write man*] I declare myself a man. Cf. note 8, page 47: "*I write* good creature."
[19]*for two ordinaries*] for two dinners, for the time spent over two dinners with you.
[20]*taking up*] There is a play here on the two meanings of this expression "buying on
credit" and "contradicting or exposing error in conversation."

which if—Lord have mercy on thee for a hen![21] So, my good window of lattice,[22] fare thee well: thy casement I need not open, for
I look through thee. Give me thy hand.

PAR.   My lord, you give me most egregious indignity.

LAF.   Ay, with all my heart; and thou art worthy of it.

PAR.   I have not, my lord, deserved it.

LAF.   Yes, good faith, every dram of it; and I will not bate thee a
scruple.

PAR.   Well, I shall be wiser.

LAF.   Ev'n as soon as thou canst, for thou hast to pull at a smack o' the
contrary. If ever thou be'st bound in thy scarf and beaten, thou
shalt find what it is to be proud of thy bondage. I have a desire to
hold my acquaintance with thee, or rather my knowledge, that I
may say in the default, he is a man I know.

PAR.   My lord, you do me most insupportable vexation.

LAF.   I would it were hell-pains for thy sake, and my poor doing eternal: for doing I am past; as I will by thee, in what motion age will
give me leave.[23]   [Exit.

PAR.   Well, thou hast a son shall take this disgrace off me; scurvy, old,
filthy, scurvy lord! Well, I must be patient; there is no fettering of
authority. I'll beat him, by my life, if I can meet him with any convenience, an he were double and double a lord. I'll have no more
pity of his age than I would have of—I'll beat him, an if I could
but meet him again.

Re-enter LAFEU

LAF.   Sirrah, your lord and master's married; there's news for you: you
have a new mistress.

PAR.   I most unfeignedly beseech your lordship to make some reservation of your wrongs: he is my good lord: whom I serve above is
my master.

LAF.   Who? God?

PAR.   Ay, sir.

LAF.   The devil it is that's thy master. Why dost thou garter up thy
arms o' this fashion? dost make hose of thy sleeves? do other servants so? Thou wert best set thy lower part where thy nose stands.
By mine honour, if I were but two hours younger, I 'ld beat thee:
methinks't, thou art a general offence, and every man should beat

[21]*a hen*] a coward. Cf. "hen-hearted," "chicken-hearted."
[22]*window of lattice*] a window with a blind that may be seen through.
[23]*for doing . . . leave*] My time of doing or action is past, so I will pass by thee (*i.e.* leave
thee) as quickly as age permits. There is a lame quibble on "past" as a participle of
"pass."

thee: I think thou wast created for men to breathe themselves upon thee.

PAR.   This is hard and undeserved measure, my lord.

LAF.   Go to, sir; you were beaten in Italy for picking a kernel out of a pomegranate; you are a vagabond, and no true traveller: you are more saucy with lords and honourable personages than the commission of your birth and virtue gives you heraldry. You are not worth another word, else I 'ld call you knave. I leave you.   [*Exit.*

PAR.   Good, very good; it is so then: good, very good; let it be concealed awhile.

Re-enter BERTRAM

BER.   Undone, and forfeited to cares for ever!

PAR.   What's the matter, sweet-heart?

BER.   Although before the solemn priest I have sworn, I will not bed her.

PAR.   What, what, sweet-heart?

BER.   O my Parolles, they have married me!
I'll to the Tuscan wars, and never bed her.

PAR.   France is a dog-hole, and it no more merits
The tread of a man's foot: to the wars!

BER.   There's letters from my mother: what the import is, I know not yet.

PAR.   Ay, that would be known. To the wars, my boy, to the wars!
He wears his honour in a box unseen,
That hugs his kicky-wicky here at home,
Spending his manly marrow in her arms,
Which should sustain the bound and high curvet
Of Mars's fiery steed. To other regions
France is a stable; we that dwell in 't jades;
Therefore, to the war!

BER.   It shall be so: I'll send her to my house,
Acquaint my mother with my hate to her,
And wherefore I am fled; write to the king
That which I durst not speak: his present gift
Shall furnish me to those Italian fields,
Where noble fellows strike: war is no strife
To the dark house and the detested wife.[24]

PAR.   Will this capriccio hold in thee, art sure?

BER.   Go with me to my chamber, and advise me.

[24]*To the dark house, etc.*] Compared with the gloomy home and the hated wife. *Detested* is Rowe's correction for *detected* of the Folios.

I'll send her straight away: to-morrow
I'll to the wars, she to her single sorrow.

PAR.   Why, these balls bound; there's noise in it.
'T is hard:[25]
A young man married is a man that's marr'd:
Therefore away, and leave her bravely; go:
The king has done you wrong: but, hush, 't is so.   [*Exeunt.*

SCENE IV. *Paris: The King's Palace.*

Enter HELENA *and* Clown

HEL.   My mother greets me kindly: is she well?

CLO.   She is not well; but yet she has her health: she's very merry; but
yet she is not well: but thanks be given, she's very well and wants
nothing i' the world; but yet she is not well.

HEL.   If she be very well, what does she ail, that she's not very well?

CLO.   Truly, she's very well indeed, but for two things.

HEL.   What two things?

CLO.   One, that she's not in heaven, whither God send her quickly!
the other, that she's in earth, from whence God send her quickly!

Enter PAROLLES

PAR.   Bless you, my fortunate lady!

HEL.   I hope, sir, I have your good will to have mine own good fortunes.

PAR.   You had my prayers to lead them on; and to keep them on, have
them still. O, my knave, how does my old lady?

CLO.   So that you had her wrinkles, and I her money, I would she did
as you say.

PAR.   Why, I say nothing.

CLO.   Marry, you are the wiser man; for many a man's tongue shakes
out his master's undoing: to say nothing, to do nothing, to know
nothing, and to have nothing, is to be a great part of your title;
which is within a very little of nothing.

PAR.   Away! thou 'rt a knave.

CLO.   You should have said, sir, before a knave thou 'rt a knave; that's,
before me thou 'rt a knave: this had been truth, sir.

PAR.   Go to, thou art a witty fool; I have found thee.

CLO.   Did you find me in yourself, sir? or were you taught to find me?

---

[25]*Why, these balls . . . hard*] Proverbial expressions meaning "This goes well."

The search, sir, was profitable; and much fool may you find in
you, even to the world's pleasure and the increase of laughter.

PAR.   A good knave, i' faith, and well fed.
Madam, my lord will go away to-night;
A very serious business calls on him.
The great prerogative and rite of love,
Which, as your due, time claims, he does acknowledge;
But puts it off to a compell'd restraint;
Whose want, and whose delay, is strew'd with sweets,
Which they distil now in the curbed time,[1]
To make the coming hour o'erflow with you,
And pleasure drown the brim.

HEL.   What's his will else?

PAR.   That you will take your instant leave o' the king,
And make this haste as your own good proceeding,
Strengthen'd with what apology you think
May make it probable need.[2]

HEL.   What more commands he?

PAR.   That, having this obtain'd, you presently
Attend his further pleasure.

HEL.   In every thing I wait upon his will.

PAR.   I shall report it so.

HEL.   I pray you. [*Exit* PAROLLES.] Come, sirrah.   [*Exeunt.*

SCENE V. *Paris: The King's Palace.*

Enter LAFEU *and* BERTRAM

LAF.   But I hope your lordship thinks not him a soldier.

BER.   Yes, my lord, and of very valiant approof.

LAF.   You have it from his own deliverance.

BER.   And by other warranted testimony.

LAF.   Then my dial goes not true: I took this lark for a bunting.[1]

BER.   I do assure you, my lord, he is very great in knowledge, and ac-
cordingly valiant.

LAF.   I have then sinned against his experience and transgressed
against his valour; and my state that way is dangerous, since I cannot yet find in my heart to repent. Here he comes: I pray you,
make us friends; I will pursue the amity.

[1]*curbed time*] the season of restraint.
[2]*make it probable need*] give it a specious appearance of necessity.

[1]*a bunting*] a bird with plumage resembling that of a lark, but without the lark's note.

Enter PAROLLES

PAR. These things shall be done, sir.   [*To* BERTRAM.
LAF. Pray you, sir, who's his tailor?
PAR. Sir?
LAF. O, I know him well, I, sir; he, sir, 's a good workman, a very good
      tailor.
BER. Is she gone to the king?   [*Aside to* PAROLLES.
PAR. She is.
BER. Will she away to-night?
PAR. As you'll have her.
BER. I have writ my letters, casketed my treasure,
      Given order for our horses; and to-night,
      When I should take possession of the bride,
      End ere I do begin.
LAF. A good traveller is something at the latter end of a dinner; but
      one that lies three thirds, and uses a known truth to pass a thou-
      sand nothings with, should be once heard, and thrice beaten. God
      save you, captain.
BER. Is there any unkindness between my lord and you, monsieur?
PAR. I know not how I have deserved to run into my lord's displeasure.
LAF. You have made shift to run into 't, boots and spurs and all, like
      him that leaped into the custard;[2] and out of it you'll run again,
      rather than suffer question for your residence.
BER. It may be you have mistaken him, my lord.
LAF. And shall do so ever, though I took him at 's prayers. Fare you
      well, my lord; and believe this of me, there can be no kernel in
      this light nut; the soul of this man is his clothes. Trust him not in
      matter of heavy consequence; I have kept of them tame, and know
      their natures. Farewell, monsieur: I have spoken better of you than
      you have or will to deserve at my hand; but we must do good
      against evil.   [*Exit.*
PAR. An idle lord, I swear.
BER. I think so.
PAR. Why, do you not know him?
BER. Yes, I do know him well, and common speech
      Gives him a worthy pass. Here comes my clog.

Enter HELENA

[2]*leaped into the custard*] At the Lord Mayor's banquets in the city of London, the city
fool was wont to leap into a custard prepared for the purpose. Cf. Ben Jonson, *The
Devil is an Ass*, I, i, 95–97:
              "He may perchance, in tale of a Sheriff's dinner,
              Skip with a rime o' the Table, from New-Nothing,
              And take his Almaine-leap into a custard."

HEL.   I have, sir, as I was commanded from you,
     Spoke with the king, and have procured his leave
     For present parting; only he desires
     Some private speech with you.
BER.   I shall obey his will.
     You must not marvel, Helen, at my course,
     Which holds not colour with the time, nor does
     The ministration and required office
     On my particular.[3] Prepared I was not
     For such a business; therefore am I found
     So much unsettled: this drives me to entreat you,
     That presently you take your way for home,
     And rather muse than ask why I entreat you;
     For my respects[4] are better than they seem,
     And my appointments have in them a need
     Greater than shows itself at the first view
     To you that know them not. This to my mother:
                              [Giving a letter.
     'T will be two days ere I shall see you; so,
     I leave you to your wisdom.
HEL.   Sir, I can nothing say,
     But that I am your most obedient servant.
BER.   Come, come, no more of that.
HEL.   And ever shall
     With true observance seek to eke out that
     Wherein toward me my homely stars have fail'd
     To equal my great fortune.
BER.   Let that go:
     My haste is very great: farewell; hie home.
HEL.   Pray, sir, your pardon.
BER.   Well, what would you say?
HEL.   I am not worthy of the wealth I owe;
     Nor dare I say 't is mine, and yet it is;
     But, like a timorous thief, most fain would steal
     What law does vouch mine own.
BER.   What would you have?
HEL.   Something; and scarce so much: nothing, indeed.
     I would not tell you what I would, my lord: faith, yes;
     Strangers and foes do sunder, and not kiss.
BER.   I pray you, stay not, but in haste to horse.
HEL.   I shall not break your bidding, good my lord.

---

[3]*On my particular*] On my part, as far as I am concerned.
[4]*respects*] reasons, motives.

BER.   Where are my other men, monsieur?[5] Farewell!

[*Exit* HELENA.

Go thou toward home; where I will never come
Whilst I can shake my sword, or hear the drum.
Away, and for our flight.

PAR.   Bravely, coragio!   [*Exeunt.*

[5]*Where are my other, etc.*] Theobald first gave this speech to Bertram. In the earlier editions it is assigned to Helena.

ACT III.

SCENE I. *Florence: The Duke's Palace.*

Flourish. Enter the DUKE *of Florence, attended; the two Frenchmen with a troop of soldiers*

DUKE.   So that from point to point now have you heard
The fundamental reasons of this war,
Whose great decision hath much blood let forth
And more thirsts after.

FIRST LORD.   Holy seems the quarrel
Upon your Grace's part; black and fearful
On the opposer.

DUKE.   Therefore we marvel much our cousin France
Would in so just a business shut his bosom
Against our borrowing prayers.[1]

SEC. LORD.   Good my lord,
The reasons of our state I cannot yield,
But like a common and an outward man,
That the great figure of a council frames
By self-unable motion:[2] therefore dare not
Say what I think of it, since I have found
Myself in my incertain grounds to fail
As often as I guess'd.

DUKE.   Be it his pleasure.

FIRST LORD.   But I am sure the younger of our nature,[3]
That surfeit on their ease, will day by day
Come here for physic.

---

[1]*borrowing prayers*] Prayers that would borrow of him assistance.
[2]*The reasons . . . motion*] I know nothing of politics, except, like any ordinary outsider, who forms some idea of what the great councillors determine by effort, which of itself is inadequate to attain full knowledge. "Self-unable motion" is "mental or physical activity which is not self-sufficing, and bears no fruit."
[3]*younger of our nature*] young men of our rank or condition.

39

DUKE. Welcome shall they be;
And all the honours that can fly from us
Shall on them settle. You know your places well;
When better fall, for your avails they fell:[4]
To-morrow to the field. [*Flourish.*

SCENE II. *Rousillon: The Count's Palace.*

Enter the COUNTESS *and* Clown

COUNT. It hath happened all as I would have had it, save that he comes not along with her.
CLO. By my troth, I take my young lord to be a very melancholy man.
COUNT. By what observance, I pray you?
CLO. Why, he will look upon his boot and sing; mend the ruff[1] and sing; ask questions and sing; pick his teeth and sing. I know a man that had this trick of melancholy sold a goodly manor for a song.
COUNT. Let me see what he writes, and when he means to come.
[*Opening a letter.*
CLO. I have no mind to Isbel since I was at court: our old ling[2] and our Isbels o' the country are nothing like your old ling and your Isbels o' the court: the brains of my Cupid's knocked out, and I begin to love, as an old man loves money, with no stomach.
COUNT. What have we here?
CLO. E'en that you have there. [*Exit.*
COUNT. [*reads*] I have sent you a daughter-in-law: she hath recovered the king, and undone me. I have wedded her, not bedded her; and sworn to make the "not" eternal. You shall hear I am run away: know it before the report come. If there be breadth enough in the world, I will hold a long distance. My duty to you.

Your unfortunate son,
BERTRAM.

This is not well, rash and unbridled boy,
To fly the favours of so good a king;

[4]*When . . . fell*] When men in higher positions fall, their fall must be to your advantage; you know the usual conditions of promotion.

[1]*the ruff*] Here used of the boot, the top edge of which often had an ornamental ruff or ruffle. Cf. Jonson's *Every Man out of his Humour*, IV, 2, *ad fin*, "*the ruffle* of my boot."
[2]*old ling*] literally, "stale salt fish, which was ordinary Lenten fare." The words may here be applied to old women. Such usage adds very little point to the clown's contrast of women of the court with those of the country. It has been ingeniously suggested that, both in this and the next line, *old ling* is a misreading of *codlings, i.e.* "raw youths."

To pluck his indignation on thy head
By the misprising³ of a maid too virtuous
For the contempt of empire.

Re-enter Clown

CLO. O madam, yonder is heavy news within between two soldiers
and my young lady!
COUNT. What is the matter?
CLO. Nay, there is some comfort in the news, some comfort; your son
will not be killed so soon as I thought he would.
COUNT. Why should he be killed:
CLO. So say I, madam, if he run away, as I hear he does: the danger
is in standing to 't; that's the loss of men, though it be the getting
of children. Here they come will tell you more: for my part, I only
hear your son was run away.   [*Exit.*

Enter HELENA *and two* Gentlemen

FIRST GENT.⁴ Save you, good madam.
HEL. Madam, my lord is gone, for ever gone.
SEC. GENT. Do not say so.
COUNT. Think upon patience. Pray you, gentlemen,
I have felt so many quirks of joy and grief,
That the first face of neither, on the start,
Can woman me unto 't:⁵ where is my son, I pray you?
SEC. GENT. Madam, he's gone to serve the duke of Florence:
We met him thitherward; for thence we came,
And, after some dispatch in hand at court,
Thither we bend again.
HEL. Look on his letter, madam; here's my passport.
[*reads*] When thou canst get the ring upon my finger which never shall
come off, and show me a child begotten of thy body that I am father to,
then call me husband: but in such a "then" I write a "never."
This is a dreadful sentence.
COUNT. Brought you this letter, gentlemen?
FIRST GENT.   Ay, madam;
And for the contents' sake are sorry for our pains.
COUNT. I prithee, lady, have a better cheer;
If thou engrossest all the griefs are thine,
Thou robb'st me of a moiety: he was my son;

³*misprising*] contemning. See note 12 on page 29.
⁴*First Gent.*] In the First Folio this character is called "French E," and the "Second
Gent." is called "French G." See note 1 on page 17.
⁵*Can woman me unto 't:*] Can make me womanlike give way to emotion.

But I do wash his name out of my blood,
And thou art all my child. Towards Florence is he?

SEC. GENT. Ay, madam.

COUNT. And to be a soldier?

SEC. GENT. Such is his noble purpose; and, believe 't,
The Duke will lay upon him all the honour
That good convenience claims.

COUNT. Return you thither?

FIRST GENT. Ay, madam, with the swiftest wing of speed.

HEL. [*reads*] Till I have no wife, I have nothing in France.
'T is bitter.

COUNT. Find you that there?

HEL. Ay, madam.

FIRST. GENT. 'T is but the boldness of his hand, haply, which his
heart was not consenting to.

COUNT. Nothing in France, until he have no wife!
There's nothing here that is too good for him
But only she; and she deserves a lord
That twenty such rude boys might tend upon
And call her hourly mistress. Who was with him?

FIRST GENT. A servant only, and a gentleman
Which I have sometime known.

COUNT. Parolles, was it not?

FIRST GENT. Ay, my good lady, he.

COUNT. A very tainted fellow, and full of wickedness.
My son corrupts a well-derived nature
With his inducement.[6]

FIRST GENT. Indeed, good lady,
The fellow has a deal of that too much,
Which holds him much to have.[7]

COUNT. Y' are welcome, gentlemen.
I will entreat you, when you see my son,
To tell him that his sword can never win
The honour that he loses: more I'll entreat you
Written to bear along.

SEC. GENT. We serve you, madam,
In that and all your worthiest affairs.

[6]*With his inducement*] Under his influence.
[7]*The fellow . . . have*] "Too much" seems to be used as a substantive in the sense of "excess" (of vanity). The meaning may be, "The fellow has a deal of that excess (of vanity) which gives him the repute of possessing an amplitude or sufficiency (of valour)." But the difficult phrase "holds him much to have" is usually reckoned to be corrupt. The suggestion "fouls him," etc., is worth attention.

COUNT.   Not so, but as we change our courtesies.[8]
    Will you draw near?
[Exeunt COUNTESS and Gentlemen.
HEL.   "Till I have no wife, I have nothing in France."
    Nothing in France, until he has no wife!
    Thou shalt have none, Rousillon, none in France;
    Then hast thou all again. Poor lord! is 't I
    That chase thee from thy country and expose
    Those tender limbs of thine to the event
    Of the none-sparing war? and is it I
    That drive thee from the sportive court, where thou
    Wast shot at with fair eyes, to be the mark
    Of smoky muskets? O you leaden messengers,
    That ride upon the violent speed of fire,
    Fly with false aim; move the still-peering air,
    That sings with piercing; do not touch my lord.[9]
    Whoever shoots at him, I set him there;
    Whoever charges on his forward breast,
    I am the caitiff that do hold him to 't;
    And, though I kill him not, I am the cause
    His death was so effected: better 't were
    I met the ravin lion when he roar'd
    With sharp constraint of hunger; better 't were
    That all the miseries which nature owes
    Were mine at once. No, come thou home, Rousillon,
    Whence honour but of danger wins a scar,
    As oft it loses all:[10] I will be gone;
    My being here it is that holds thee hence:
    Shall I stay here to do 't? no, no, although
    The air of paradise did fan the house,
    And angels officed all: I will be gone,
    That pitiful rumour may report my flight,
    To consolate thine ear. Come, night; end, day!
    For with the dark, poor thief, I'll steal away.   [*Exit.*

---

[8]*change our courtesies*] exchange or reciprocate civilities.
[9]*the still-peering air . . . lord*] "Disturb or cut through the still, quiet air, which makes a singing or hissing sound as the bullet pierces it; (take any course, do anything, but) do not touch my lord." "Still-peering" is an emphatic amplification of "still," *i.e.* quiet. "Peer" is frequently used for "appear," or "seen." The epithet is equivalent to "still seeming," "silent to all appearance."
[10]*come . . . all*] come home from that place where the quest of honour gets at most out of a dangerous adventure nothing but a scar, while it as often loses everything.

SCENE III. *Florence: Before the Duke's Palace.*

Flourish. Enter the DUKE *of Florence,* BERTRAM, PAROLLES, Soldiers, Drum, *and* Trumpets

DUKE.   The general of our horse thou art; and we,
        Great in our hope, lay our best love and credence
        Upon thy promising fortune.
BER.   Sir, it is
        A charge too heavy for my strength; but yet
        We'll strive to bear it for your worthy sake
        To the extreme edge of hazard.
DUKE.   Then go thou forth;
        And fortune play upon thy prosperous helm,
        As thy auspicious mistress!
BER.   This very day,
        Great Mars, I put myself into thy file:
        Make me but like my thoughts, and I shall prove
        A lover of thy drum, hater of love.   [*Exeunt.*

SCENE IV. *Rousillon: The Count's Palace.*

Enter the COUNTESS *and* Steward

COUNT.   Alas! and would you take the letter of her?
        Might you not know she would do as she has done,
        By sending me a letter? Read it again.
STEW. [*reads*]   I am Saint Jaques' pilgrim,[1] thither gone:
            Ambitious love hath so in me offended,
        That barefoot plod I the cold ground upon,
            With sainted vow my faults to have amended.
        Write, write, that from the bloody course of war
            My dearest master, your dear son, may hie:
        Bless him at home in peace, whilst I from far
            His name with zealous fervour sanctify:
        His taken labours bid him me forgive;
            I, his despiteful Juno, sent him forth
        From courtly friends with camping foes to live,
            Where death and danger dogs the heels of worth:
        He is too good and fair for death and me;
            Whom I myself embrace to set him free.

[1]*Saint Jaques' pilgrim*] Shakespeare invented the reference to Saint Jaques (Saint James the Greater), but gives no precise indication as to which of the many shrines of the saint Helena pretends to make pilgrimage. She subsequently calls the saint "Jaques le Grand" and "great Saint Jaques," pages 46 and 48.

COUNT.   Ah, what sharp stings are in her mildest words!
    Rinaldo, you did never lack advice so much,
    As letting her pass so: had I spoke with her,
    I could have well diverted her intents,
    Which thus she hath prevented.
STEW.   Pardon me, madam:
    If I had given you this at over-night,
    She might have been o'erta'en; and yet she writes,
    Pursuit would be but vain.
COUNT.   What angel shall
    Bless this unworthy husband? he cannot thrive,
    Unless her prayers, whom heaven delights to hear
    And loves to grant, reprieve him from the wrath
    Of greatest justice. Write, write, Rinaldo,
    To this unworthy husband of his wife;
    Let every word weigh heavy of her worth
    That he does weigh too light: my greatest grief,
    Though little he do feel it, set down sharply.
    Dispatch the most convenient messenger:
    When haply he shall hear that she is gone,
    He will return; and hope I may that she,
    Hearing so much, will speed her foot again,
    Led hither by pure love: which of them both
    Is dearest to me, I have no skill in sense
    To make distinction: provide this messenger:
    My heart is heavy and mine age is weak;
    Grief would have tears, and sorrow bids me speak.   [*Exeunt.*

SCENE V. *Florence: Without the Walls. A tucket afar off.*

Enter an old Widow *of Florence,* DIANA, VIOLENTA, *and* MARIANA, *with other* Citizens

WID.   Nay, come; for if they do approach the city, we shall lose all the sight.
DIA.   They say[1] the French count has done most honourable service.
WID.   It is reported that he has taken their greatest commander; and that with his own hand he slew the Duke's brother. [*Tucket.*] We have lost our labour; they are gone a contrary way: hark! you may know by their trumpets.

[1]*They say, etc.*] The Cambridge editors assign this speech to Violenta, who, though mentioned in the stage direction, does not figure among the speakers in the old editions.

MAR.   Come, let's return again, and suffice ourselves with the report
of it. Well, Diana, take heed of this French earl: the honour of a
maid is her name; and no legacy is so rich as honesty.

WID.   I have told my neighbour how you have been solicited by a gentleman his companion.

MAR.   I know that knave; hang him! one Parolles: a filthy officer he is
in those suggestions for the young earl. Beware of them, Diana;
their promises, enticements, oaths, tokens, and all these engines of
lust, are not the things they go under:[2] many a maid hath been se-
duced by them; and the misery is, example, that so terrible shows
in the wreck of maidenhood, cannot for all that dissuade succession,[3] but that they are limed with the twigs[4] that threaten them. I
hope I need not to advise you further; but I hope your own grace
will keep you where you are, though there were no further danger
known but the modesty which is so lost.

DIA.   You shall not need to fear me.

WID.   I hope so.

Enter HELENA, *disguised like a Pilgrim*

Look, here comes a pilgrim: I know she will lie at my house;
thither they send one another: I'll question her. God save you, pilgrim! whither are you bound?

HEL.   To Saint Jaques le Grand.
Where do the palmers lodge, I do beseech you?

WID.   At the Saint Francis here beside the port.

HEL.   Is this the way?

WID.   Ay, marry, is 't. [*A march afar.*] Hark you! they come this way.
If you will tarry, holy pilgrim,
But till the troops come by,
I will conduct you where you shall be lodged;
The rather, for I think I know your hostess
As ample[5] as myself.

HEL.   Is it yourself?

WID.   If you shall please so, pilgrim.

HEL.   I thank you, and will stay upon your leisure.

WID.   You came, I think, from France?

HEL.   I did so.

---

[2]*go under*] pass for, profess to be.

[3]*dissuade succession*] dissuade from following the same track.

[4]*limed with the twigs*] ensnared with the twigs, as in hunting wild animals. Cf. note 6,
page 51.

[5]*ample*] fully, well.

WID.   Here you shall see a countryman of yours
   That has done worthy service.
HEL.   His name, I pray you?
DIA. The Count Rousillon: know you such a one?
HEL. But by the ear, that hears most nobly of him:
   His face I know not.
DIA.   Whatsome'er he is,
   He's bravely taken[6] here. He stole from France,
   As 't is reported, for the king had married him
   Against his liking: think you it is so?
HEL. Ay, surely, mere the truth:[7] I know his lady.
DIA. There is a gentleman that serves the count
   Reports but coarsely of her.
HEL.   What's his name?
DIA. Monsieur Parolles.
HEL.   O, I believe with him,
   In argument of praise, or to the worth
   Of the great count himself, she is too mean
   To have her name repeated: all her deserving
   Is a reserved honesty, and that
   I have not heard examined.
DIA.   Alas, poor lady!
   'T is a hard bondage to become the wife
   Of a detesting lord.
WID. I write good creature,[8] wheresoe'er she is,
   Her heart weighs sadly: this young maid might do her
   A shrewd turn, if she pleased.
HEL.   How do you mean?
   May be the amorous count solicits her
   In the unlawful purpose.
WID.   He does indeed;
   And brokes[9] with all that can in such a suit
   Corrupt the tender honour of a maid:
   But she is arm'd for him, and keeps her guard
   In honestest defence.
MAR.   The gods forbid else!

[6]*He's bravely taken*] He is held in high esteem.
[7]*mere the truth*] absolutely true.
[8]*I write good creature*] I declare her to be good creature. Cf. note 18, page 30, "*I write
 man.*" *I write* is the First Folio reading for which *I right* [*i.e.* Ay, right;] *good creature* is
 substituted in the Second and later Folios and has been adopted by most eighteenth
 and nineteenth century editors.
[9]*brokes*] trades, acts as broker or pander.

WID.   So, now they come:

Drum and Colours
Enter BERTRAM, PAROLLES, *and the whole army*

    That is Antonio, the Duke's eldest son;
    That, Escalus.
HEL.   Which is the Frenchman?
DIA.   He;
    That with the plume: 't is a most gallant fellow.
    I would he loved his wife: if he were honester
    He were much goodlier: is 't not a handsome gentleman?
HEL.   I like him well.
DIA.   'T is pity he is not honest: yond 's that same knave
    That leads him to these places: were I his lady,
    I would poison that vile rascal.
HEL.   Which is he?
DIA.   That jack-an-apes with scarfs: why is he melancholy?
HEL.   Perchance he's hurt i' the battle.
PAR.   Lose our drum! well.
MAR.   He's shrewdly vexed at something: look, he has spied us.
WID.   Marry, hang you!
MAR.   And your courtesy, for a ring-carrier![10]
                    [*Exeunt* BERTRAM, PAROLLES, *and army.*
WID.   The troop is past. Come, pilgrim, I will bring you
    Where you shall host: of enjoin'd penitents[11]
    There's four or five, to great Saint Jaques bound,
    Already at my house.
HEL.   I humbly thank you:
    Please it this matron and this gentle maid
    To eat with us to-night, the charge and thanking
    Shall be for me; and, to requite you further,
    I will bestow some precepts of this virgin
    Worthy the note.
BOTH.   We'll take your offer kindly.
                                [*Exeunt.*

---

[10]*ring-carrier*] pander, bawd.
[11]*enjoin'd penitents*] persons under a vow of doing penance.

Scene VI. *Camp before Florence.*

Enter BERTRAM *and the two French* Lords

SEC. LORD.[1]   Nay, good my lord, put him to 't; let him have his way.

FIRST LORD.   If your lordship find him not a hilding, hold me no more in your respect.

SEC. LORD.   On my life, my lord, a bubble.

BER.   Do you think I am so far deceived in him?

SEC. LORD.   Believe it, my lord, in mine own direct knowledge, without any malice, but to speak of him as my kinsman, he's a most notable coward, an infinite and endless liar, an hourly promise-breaker, the owner of no one good quality worthy your lordship's entertainment.

FIRST LORD.   It were fit you knew him; lest, reposing too far in his virtue, which he hath not, he might at some great and trusty business in a main danger fail you.

BER.   I would I knew in what particular action to try him.

FIRST LORD.   None better than to let him fetch off his drum, which you hear him so confidently undertake to do.

SEC. LORD.   I, with a troop of Florentines, will suddenly surprise him; such I will have, whom I am sure he knows not from the enemy: we will bind and hoodwink him so, that he shall suppose no other but that he is carried into the leaguer of the adversaries, when we bring him to our own tents. Be but your lordship present at his examination: if he do not, for the promise of his life and in the highest compulsion of base fear, offer to betray you and deliver all the intelligence in his power against you, and that with the divine forfeit of his soul upon oath, never trust my judgement in any thing.

FIRST LORD.   O, for the love of laughter, let him fetch his drum; he says he has a stratagem for 't: when your lordship sees the bottom of his success in 't, and to what metal this counterfeit lump of ore will be melted, if you give him not John Drum's entertainment,[2] your inclining cannot be removed. Here he comes.

Enter PAROLLES

---

[1]*Sec. Lord*] In the first Folio this character is called "Cap. E" and the "First Lord" is called "Cap. G." See note 1 on page 17.

[2]*give him John Drum's entertainment*] give him a good beating. The phrase is common. Cf. Edward Aston's translation of Boemus' *Manners and Customs of all Nations*, 1611: "some others on the contrarie part, give them *John Drum's intertainm^t* reviling and beating them away from their houses."

SEC. LORD. [*Aside to* BER.] O, for the love of laughter, hinder not the honour of his design: let him fetch off his drum in any hand.[3]

BER. How now, monsieur! this drum sticks sorely in your disposition.

FIRST LORD. A pox on 't, let it go; 't is but a drum.

PAR. "But a drum"! is 't "but a drum"? A drum so lost! There was excellent command,—to charge in with our horse upon our own wings, and to rend our own soldiers!

FIRST LORD. That was not to be blamed in the command of the service: it was a disaster of war that Cæsar himself could not have prevented, if he had been there to command.

BER. Well, we cannot greatly condemn our success: some dishonour we had in the loss of that drum; but it is not to be recovered.

PAR. It might have been recovered.

BER. It might; but it is not now.

PAR. It is to be recovered: but that the merit of service is seldom attributed to the true and exact performer, I would have that drum or another, or "hic jacet."

BER. Why, if you have a stomach, to 't, monsieur: if you think your mystery in stratagem can bring this instrument of honour again into his native quarter, be magnanimous in the enterprise and go on; I will grace the attempt for a worthy exploit: if you speed well in it, the Duke shall both speak of it, and extend to you what further becomes his greatness, even to the utmost syllable of your worthiness.

PAR. By the hand of a soldier, I will undertake it.

BER. But you must not now slumber in it.

PAR. I'll about it this evening: and I will presently pen down my dilemmas,[4] encourage myself in my certainty, put myself into my mortal preparation; and by midnight look to hear further from me.

BER. May I be bold to acquaint his Grace you are gone about it?

PAR. I know not what the success will be, my lord; but the attempt I vow.

BER. I know thou 'rt valiant; and, to the possibility of thy soldiership, will subscribe for thee. Farewell.

PAR. I love not many words. [*Exit.*

SEC. LORD. No more than a fish loves water. Is not this a strange fellow, my lord, that so confidently seems to undertake this business, which he knows is not to be done; damns himself to do, and dares better be damned than to do 't?

FIRST LORD. You do not know him, my lord, as we do: certain it is, that he will steal himself into a man's favour and for a week escape

---

[3]*in any hand*] in any case, at any rate.
[4]*dilemmas*] the various difficulties of the undertaking.

a great deal of discoveries; but when you find him out, you have
him ever after.

BER.   Why, do you think he will make no deed at all of this that so seriously he does address himself unto?

SEC. LORD.   None in the world; but return with an invention, and
clap upon you two or three probable lies: but we have almost embossed[5] him; you shall see his fall to-night; for indeed he is not for
your lordship's respect.

FIRST LORD.   We'll make you some sport with the fox ere we case him.
He was first smoked by the old lord Lafeu: when his disguise and
he is parted, tell me what a sprat you shall find him; which you
shall see this very night.

SEC. LORD.   I must go look my twigs:[6] he shall be caught.

BER.   Your brother he shall go along with me.

SEC. LORD.   As 't please your lordship: I'll leave you.   [Exit.

BER.   Now will I lead you to the house, and show you
The lass I spoke of.

FIRST LORD.   But you say she's honest.

BER.   That's all the fault: I spoke with her but once
And found her wondrous cold; but I sent to her,
By this same coxcomb that we have i' the wind,
Tokens and letters which she did re-send;
And this is all I have done. She's a fair creature:
Will you go see her?

FIRST LORD.   With all my heart, my lord.   [Exeunt.

SCENE VII. *Florence: The Widow's House.*

Enter HELENA *and* Widow

HEL.   If you misdoubt me that I am not she,
I know not how I shall assure you further,
But I shall lose the grounds I work upon.[1]

WID.   Though my estate be fallen, I was well born,
Nothing acquainted with these businesses;

---

[5]*embossed*] used of a hunted animal driven to extremities. Cf. Spenser, *Fairy Queen*, III,
i, 21: "The savage beast *embossed* in weary chase."

[6]*I must go look my twigs*] Cf. note 4, page 46: "They are limed [*i.e.* ensnared] with *the
twigs.*"

---

[1]*But I . . . upon*] Unless I forfeit my present aim (which is to conceal my identity from
Bertram).

And would not put my reputation now
In any staining act.
HEL.   Nor would I wish you.
First, give me trust, the count he is my husband,
And what to your sworn counsel I have spoken
Is so from word to word; and then you cannot,
By the good aid that I of you shall borrow,
Err in bestowing it.
WID.   I should believe you;
For you have show'd me that which well approves
You're great in fortune.
HEL.   Take this purse of gold,
And let me buy your friendly help thus far,
Which I will over-pay and pay again
When I have found it. The count he wooes your daughter,
Lays down his wanton siege before her beauty,
Resolved to carry her: let her in fine consent,
As we'll direct her how 't is best to bear it.
Now his important blood[2] will nought deny
That she'll demand: a ring the county wears,
That downward hath succeeded in his house
From son to son, some four or five descents
Since the first father wore it: this ring he holds
In most rich choice; yet in his idle fire,
To buy his will, it would not seem too dear,
Howe'er repented after.
WID.   Now I see
The bottom of your purpose.
HEL.   You see it lawful, then: it is no more,
But that your daughter, ere she seems as won,
Desires this ring; appoints him an encounter;
In fine, delivers me to fill the time,
Herself most chastely absent: after this,
To marry her, I'll add three thousand crowns
To what is past already.
WID.   I have yielded:
Instruct my daughter how she shall persever,
That time and place with this deceit so lawful
May prove coherent. Every night he comes
With musics of all sorts and songs composed
To her unworthiness: it nothing steads us

---

[2]*important blood*] importunate blood.

>   To chide him from our eaves; for he persists
>   As if his life lay on 't.
> HEL.   Why then to-night
>   Let us essay our plot; which, if it speed,
>   Is wicked meaning in a lawful deed,
>   And lawful meaning in a lawful act,
>   Where both not sin, and yet a sinful fact:[3]
>   But let's about it.   [*Exeunt.*

---

[3]*both . . . a sinful fact*] both parties are free from sin; and yet the deed is rendered sinful by the attendant deception and mystification.

ACT IV.

SCENE I. *Without the Florentine Camp.*

Enter Second French Lord, *with five or six other* Soldiers *in ambush*

SECOND LORD.   We can come no other way but by this hedge-corner. When you sally upon him, speak what terrible language you will: though you understand it not yourselves, no matter; for we must not seem to understand him, unless some one among us whom we must produce for an interpreter.

FIRST SOLD.   Good captain, let me be the interpreter.

SEC. LORD.   Art not acquainted with him? knows he not thy voice?

FIRST SOLD.   No, sir, I warrant you.

SEC. LORD.   But what linsey-woolsey[1] hast thou to speak to us again?

FIRST SOLD.   E'en such as you speak to me.

SEC. LORD.   He must think us some band of strangers i' the adversary's entertainment. Now he hath a smack of all neighbouring languages; therefore we must every one be a man of his own fancy, not to know what we speak one to another; so we seem to know, is to know straight our purpose: choughs' language, gabble enough,[2] and good enough. As for you, interpreter, you must seem very politic. But couch, ho! here he comes, to beguile two hours in a sleep, and then to return and swear the lies he forges.

Enter PAROLLES

PAR.   Ten o'clock: within these three hours 't will be time enough to go home. What shall I say I have done? It must be a very plausive invention that carries it: they begin to smoke me; and disgraces have of late knocked too often at my door. I find my tongue is too foolhardy; but my heart hath the fear of Mars before it and of his creatures, not daring[3] the reports of my tongue.

[1] *linsey-woolsey*] gibberish. Cf. note 2, below: "choughs' language, gabble enough."
[2] *gabble enough*] more gibberish.
[3] *not daring*] putting no reliance in.

55

SEC. LORD. This is the first truth that e'er thine own tongue was guilty of.

PAR. What the devil should move me to undertake the recovery of this drum, being not ignorant of the impossibility, and knowing I had no such purpose? I must give myself some hurts, and say I got them in exploit: yet slight ones will not carry it; they will say, "Came you off with so little?" and great ones I dare not give. Wherefore, what's the instance? Tongue, I must put you into a butter-woman's mouth, and buy myself another of Bajazet's mule,[4] if you prattle me into these perils.

SEC. LORD. Is it possible he should know what he is, and be that he is?

PAR. I would the cutting of my garments would serve the turn, or the breaking of my Spanish sword.

SEC. LORD. We cannot afford you so.

PAR. Or the baring of my beard; and to say it was in stratagem.

SEC. LORD. 'T would not do.

PAR. Or to drown my clothes, and say I was stripped.

SEC. LORD. Hardly serve.

PAR. Though I swore I leaped from the window of the citadel—

SEC. LORD. How deep?

PAR. Thirty fathom.

SEC. LORD. Three great oaths would scarce make that be believed.

PAR. I would I had any drum of the enemy's: I would swear I recovered it.

SEC. LORD. You shall hear one anon.

PAR. A drum now of the enemy's,—   [*Alarum within.*

SEC. LORD. Throca movousus, cargo, cargo, cargo.

ALL. Cargo, cargo, cargo, villianda par corbo, cargo.

PAR. O, ransom, ransom! do not hide mine eyes.
        [*They seize and blindfold him.*

FIRST SOLD. Boskos thromuldo boskos.

PAR. I know you are the Muskos' regiment;
And I shall lose my life for want of language:
If there be here German, or Dane, low Dutch,
Italian, or French, let him speak to me; I'll
Discover that which shall undo the Florentine.

FIRST SOLD. Boskos vauvado: I understand thee, and can speak thy

[4]*mule*] This is the old reading, for which *mute* was substituted by Hanmer. But "mule" is often used as a synonym for "dumbness," and may well stand. The general meaning seems to be that Parolles will have to give his tongue away to a chattering butter-woman, and get another that won't speak at all, if his tongue be likely to get him into more difficulties of the kind that he is now experiencing. No other precise reference to "Bajazet's mule" or to "Bajazet's mute" has been found.

tongue. Kerelybonto, sir, betake thee to thy faith, for seventeen poniards are at thy bosom.

PAR.   O!

FIRST SOLD.   O, pray, pray, pray! Manka revania dulche.

SEC. LORD.   Oscorbidulchos volivorco.

FIRST SOLD.   The general is content to spare thee yet;
And, hoodwink'd as thou art, will lead thee on
To gather from thee: haply thou mayst inform
Something to save thy life.

PAR.   O, let me live!
And all the secrets of our camp I'll show,
Their force, their purposes; nay, I'll speak that
Which you will wonder at.

FIRST SOLD.   But wilt thou faithfully?

PAR.   If I do not, damn me.

FIRST SOLD.   Acordo linta.
Come on; thou art granted space.

               [*Exit, with* PAROLLES *guarded. A short alarum within.*

SEC. LORD.   Go, tell the Count Rousillon, and my brother,
We have caught the woodcock, and will keep him muffled
Till we do hear from them.

SEC. SOLD.   Captain, I will.

SEC. LORD.   A' will betray us all unto ourselves:
Inform on that.

SEC. SOLD.   So I will, sir.

SEC. LORD.   Till then I'll keep him dark and safely lock'd.

                                  [*Exeunt.*

SCENE II. *Florence: The Widow's House.*

Enter BERTRAM *and* DIANA

BER.   They told me that your name was Fontibell.

DIA.   No, my good lord, Diana.

BER.   Titled goddess;
And worth it, with addition! But, fair soul,
In your fine frame hath love no quality?
If the quick fire of youth light not your mind,
You are no maiden, but a monument:
When you are dead, you should be such a one
As you are now, for you are cold and stern;
And now you should be as your mother was
When your sweet self was got.

DIA.   She then was honest.

BER.   So should you be.
DIA.   No:
    My mother did but duty; such, my lord,
    As you owe to your wife.
BER.   No more o' that;
    I prithee, do not strive against my vows:[1]
    I was compell'd to her; but I love thee
    By love's own sweet constraint, and will for ever
    Do thee all rights of service.
DIA.   Ay, so you serve us
    Till we serve you; but when you have our roses,
    You barely[2] leave our thorns to prick ourselves,
    And mock us with our bareness.
BER.   How have I sworn!
DIA.   'T is not the many oaths that makes the truth,
    But the plain single vow that is vow'd true.
    What is not holy, that we swear not by,
    But take the High'st to witness: then, pray you, tell me,
    If I should swear by Jove's great attributes,
    I loved you dearly, would you believe my oaths,
    When I did love you ill? This has no holding,
    To swear by him whom I protest to love,
    That I will work against him:[3] therefore your oaths
    Are words and poor conditions, but unseal'd,
    At least in my opinion.
BER.   Change it, change it;
    Be not so holy-cruel: love is holy;
    And my integrity ne'er knew the crafts
    That you do charge men with. Stand no more off,
    But give thyself unto my sick desires,
    Who then recover: say thou art mine, and ever
    My love as it begins shall so persever.
DIA.   I see that men make rope's in such a scarre
    That we'll forsake ourselves.[4] Give me that ring.

[1]*my vows*] my vows to renounce my wife.
[2]*barely*] in their bareness.
[3]*When I did . . . work against him*] When I loved you to your dishonour and injury.
There is no sense, no consistency, in taking an oath, in the name of him whom I
protest to love, to do him a wrong.
[4]*I see that men . . . ourselves*] This is the difficult reading of the First and Second Folios;
ropes is substituted for *rope's* in the Third Folio. The general intention of the sentence is
that men prove so persuasive that women abandon their virtue without demur. "Scarre"
means "ravine," and there would seem to be some reference to making a bridge or lad-
der of ropes over a difficult pass, and so to making a dangerous situation alluringly facile.
Numerous emendations have been suggested, but none are satisfactory.

BER.   I'll lend it thee, my dear; but have no power
    To give it from me.
DIA.   Will you not, my lord?
BER.   It is an honour 'longing to our house,
    Bequeathed down from many ancestors;
    Which were the greatest obloquy i' the world
    In me to lose.
DIA.   Mine honour's such a ring:
    My chastity's the jewel of our house,
    Bequeathed down from many ancestors;
    Which were the greatest obloquy i' the world
    In me to lose: thus your own proper wisdom
    Brings in the champion Honour on my part,
    Against your vain assault.
BER.   Here, take my ring:
    My house, mine honour, yea, my life, be thine,
    And I'll be bid by thee.
DIA.   When midnight comes, knock at my chamber-window:
    I'll order take my mother shall not hear.
    Now will I charge you in the band of truth,
    When you have conquer'd my yet maiden bed,
    Remain there but an hour, nor speak to me:
    My reasons are most strong; and you shall know them
    When back again this ring shall be deliver'd:
    And on your finger in the night I'll put
    Another ring, that what in time proceeds
    May token to the future our past deeds.
    Adieu, till then; then, fail not. You have won
    A wife of me, though there my hope be done.
BER.   A heaven on earth I have won by wooing thee.   [Exit.
DIA.   For which live long to thank both heaven and me!
    You may so in the end.
    My mother told me just how he would woo,
    As if she sat in 's heart; she says all men
    Have the like oaths: he had sworn to marry me
    When his wife's dead; therefore I'll lie with him
    When I am buried. Since Frenchmen are so braid,[5]
    Marry that will, I live and die a maid:
    Only in this disguise I think 't no sin
    To cozen him that would unjustly win.   [Exit.

[5]*braid*] deceitful, tricky. The adjective is unknown elsewhere. A substantive "braid" is
often found in the sense of trick. Cf. Greene's *Never too Late* (1592): "love's *braids*"
(*i.e.* deceits). "Braidieness," *i.e.* deceitfulness, appears in Montgomerie, *Poems*, 1600.

SCENE III. *The Florentine Camp.*

Enter the two French Lords *and some two or three* Soldiers

FIRST LORD.[1]   You have not given him his mother's letter?

SEC. LORD.   I have delivered it an hour since: there is something in 't that stings his nature; for on the reading it he changed almost into another man.

FIRST LORD.   He has much worthy blame laid upon him for shaking off so good a wife and so sweet a lady.

SEC. LORD.   Especially he hath incurred the everlasting displeasure of the king, who had even tuned his bounty to sing happiness to him. I will tell you a thing, but you shall let it dwell darkly with you.

FIRST LORD.   When you have spoken it, 't is dead, and I am the grave of it.

SEC. LORD.   He hath perverted a young gentlewoman here in Florence, of a most chaste renown; and this night he fleshes his will in the spoil of her honour: he hath given her his monumental ring, and thinks himself made in the unchaste composition.[2]

FIRST LORD.   Now, God delay our rebellion![3] as we are ourselves, what things are we!

SEC. LORD.   Merely our own traitors. And as in the common course of all treasons, we still see them reveal themselves, till they attain to their abhorred ends,[4] so he that in this action contrives against his own nobility, in his proper stream o'erflows himself.[5]

FIRST LORD.   Is it not meant damnable in us, to be trumpeters of our unlawful intents? We shall not then have his company to-night?

SEC. LORD.   Not till after midnight; for he is dieted to his hour.[6]

FIRST LORD.   That approaches apace: I would gladly have him see his company anatomized, that he might take a measure of his own judgements, wherein so curiously he had set this counterfeit.[7]

[1]*First Lord*] In the Folios the "First Lord" is called "Cap. G," and the Second Lord "Cap. E." See note 1, page 17.

[2]*composition*] compact.

[3]*God delay our rebellion*] God retard or mitigate our tendency to rebel, or sin. Cf. "Natural *rebellion* done i' the blaze of youth," page 76. "Delay" has often the sense of "allay."

[4]*till they attain to their abhorred ends*] till they reach or reap their ignominious punishments.

[5]*in his . . . o'erflows himself*] blabs his secrets in his own stream (of talk), "reveals himself."

[6]*he is dieted to his hour*] he has food or work prescribed for him within the appointed hour. Diana has bidden him remain with her "but an hour," page 59.

[7]*counterfeit*] false coin, impostor.

SEC. LORD.   We will not meddle with him till he come; for his presence must be the whip of the other.

FIRST LORD.   In the meantime, what hear you of these wars?

SEC. LORD.   I hear there is an overture of peace.

FIRST LORD.   Nay, I assure you, a peace concluded.

SEC. LORD.   What will Count Rousillon do then? will he travel
higher,[8] or return again into France?

FIRST LORD.   I perceive, by this demand, you are not altogether of his
council.

SEC. LORD.   Let it be forbid, sir; so should I be a great deal of his act.

FIRST LORD.   Sir, his wife some two months since fled from his house:
her pretence is a pilgrimage to Saint Jaques le Grand; which holy
undertaking with most austere sanctimony she accomplished;
and, there residing, the tenderness of her nature became as a prey
to her grief; in fine, made a groan of her last breath, and now she
sings in heaven.

SEC. LORD.   How is this justified?

FIRST LORD.   The stronger part of it by her own letters, which makes
her story true, even to the point of her death: her death itself,
which could not be her office to say is come, was faithfully confirmed by the rector of the place.

SEC. LORD.   Hath the count all this intelligence?

FIRST LORD.   Ay, and the particular confirmations, point from point,
to the full arming of the verity.

SEC. LORD.   I am heartily sorry that he'll be glad of this.

FIRST LORD.   How mightily sometimes we make us comforts of our
losses!

SEC. LORD.   And how mightily some other times we drown our gain
in tears! The great dignity that his valour hath here acquired for
him shall at home be encountered with a shame as ample.

FIRST LORD.   The web of our life is of a mingled yarn, good and ill together: our virtues would be proud, if our faults whipped them
not; and our crimes would despair, if they were not cherished by
our virtues.

Enter a Messenger

How now! where's your master!

SERV.   He met the Duke in the street, sir, of whom he hath taken a
solemn leave: his lordship will next morning for France. The
Duke hath offered him letters of commendations to the king.

SEC. LORD.   They shall be no more than needful there, if they were
more than they can commend.

[8]*higher*] further inland.

FIRST LORD.   They cannot be too sweet for the king's tartness. Here's
his lordship now.

Enter BERTRAM

How now, my lord! is 't not after midnight?

BER.   I have to-night dispatched sixteen businesses, a month's length
a-piece, by an abstract of success:[9] I have congied with the Duke,
done my adieu with his nearest; buried a wife, mourned for her;
writ to my lady mother I am returning; entertained my convoy;[10]
and between these main parcels of dispatch effected many nicer
needs: the last was the greatest, but that I have not ended yet.

SEC. LORD.   If the business be of any difficulty, and this morning your
departure hence, it requires haste of your lordship.

BER.   I mean, the business is not ended, as fearing to hear of it hereafter. But shall we have this dialogue between the fool and the soldier? Come, bring forth this counterfeit module,[11] has deceived
me, like a double-meaning prophesier.

SEC. LORD.   Bring him forth: has sat i' the stocks all night, poor gallant knave.

BER.   No matter; his heels have deserved it, in usurping his spurs so
long.[12] How does he carry himself?

SEC. LORD.   I have told your lordship already, the stocks carry him.
But to answer you as you would be understood; he weeps like a
wench that had shed her milk: he hath confessed himself to
Morgan, whom he supposes to be a friar, from the time of his remembrance to this very instant disaster of his setting i' the stocks:
and what think you he hath confessed?

BER.   Nothing of me, has a'?

SEC. LORD.   His confession is taken, and it shall be read to his face: if
your lordship be in 't, as I believe you are, you must have the patience to hear it.

Enter PAROLLES *guarded, and* First Soldier

BER.   A plague upon him! muffled! he can say nothing of me: hush,
hush!

FIRST LORD.   Hoodman comes![13] Portotartarossa.

FIRST SOLD.   He calls for the tortures: what will you say without 'em?

[9]*by an abstract of success*] summarily, in rapid succession, without any pause.
[10]*entertained my convoy*] engaged my guides, escort.
[11]*module*] mould, model or copy, used contemptuously.
[12]*usurping . . . long*] A soldier convicted of cowardice was forcibly deprived of his spurs.
[13]*Hoodman comes!*] The cry of players at blind man's buff.

PAR.   I will confess what I know without constraint: if ye pinch me like
a pasty, I can say no more.

FIRST SOLD.   Bosko chimurcho.

FIRST LORD.   Boblibindo chicurmurco.

FIRST SOLD.   You are a merciful general. Our general bids you answer
to what I shall ask you out of a note.

PAR.   And truly, as I hope to live.

FIRST SOLD. [*reads*]   First demand of him how many horse the Duke is
strong. What say you to that?

PAR.   Five or six thousand; but very weak and unserviceable: the
troops are all scattered, and the commanders very poor rogues,
upon my reputation and credit, and as I hope to live.

FIRST SOLD.   Shall I set down your answer so?

PAR.   Do: I'll take the sacrament on 't, how and which way you will.

BER.   All's one to him. What a past-saving slave is this!

FIRST LORD.   You're deceived, my lord: this is Monsieur Parolles, the
gallant militarist,—that was his own phrase,—that had the whole
theoric of war in the knot of his scarf, and the practice in the
chape of his dagger.[14]

SEC. LORD.   I will never trust a man again for keeping his sword
clean, nor believe he can have every thing in him by wearing his
apparel neatly.

FIRST SOLD.   Well, that's set down.

PAR.   Five or six thousand horse, I said,—I will say true,—or there-
abouts, set down, for I'll speak truth.

FIRST LORD.   He's very near the truth in this.

BER.   But I con him no thanks for 't, in the nature he delivers it.

PAR.   Poor rogues, I pray you, say.

FIRST SOLD.   Well, that's set down.

PAR.   I humbly thank you, sir: a truth's a truth, the rogues are marvel-
lous poor.

FIRST SOLD. [*reads*]   Demand of him, of what strength they are a-foot. What
say you to that?

PAR.   By my troth, sir, if I were to live this present hour, I will tell true.
Let me see: Spurio, a hundred and fifty; Sebastian, so many;
Corambus, so many; Jaques, so many; Guiltian, Cosmo,
Lodowick, and Gratii, two hundred and fifty each; mine own com-
pany, Chitopher, Vaumond, Bentii, two hundred and fifty each: so
that the muster-file, rotten and sound, upon my life, amounts not

---

[14]*the whole theoric . . . dagger*] "Theorique (*i.e.* theory) and practice of warre" is a phrase
commonly met with, and is the title of a book translated from the Spanish by Sir
Edward Hoby (1597). The "chape" of the dagger was correctly the metal point at the
end of the scabbard, but here seems used for the scabbard itself.

to fifteen thousand poll; half of the which dare not shake the snow
from off their cassocks, lest they shake themselves to pieces.

BER.   What shall be done to him?

FIRST LORD.   Nothing, but let him have thanks. Demand of him my
condition, and what credit I have with the Duke.

FIRST SOLD.   Well, that's set down. [*Reads*] You shall demand of him,
whether one Captain Dumain be i' the camp, a Frenchman; what his
reputation is with the Duke; what his valour, honesty, and expertness in
wars; or whether he thinks it were not possible, with well-weighing sums
of gold, to corrupt him to a revolt. What say you to this? what do you
know of it?

PAR.   I beseech you, let me answer to the particular of the inter'gato-
ries: demand them singly.

FIRST SOLD.   Do you know this Captain Dumain?

PAR.   I know him: a' was a botcher's 'prentice in Paris, from whence
he was whipped for getting the shrieve's fool[15] with child, —a
dumb innocent, that could not say him nay.

BER.   Nay, by your leave, hold your hands; though I know his brains
are forfeit to the next tile that falls.[16]

FIRST SOLD.   Well, is this captain in the Duke of Florence's camp?

PAR.   Upon my knowledge, he is, and lousy.

FIRST LORD.   Nay, look not so upon me; we shall hear of your lordship
anon.

FIRST SOLD.   What is his reputation with the Duke?

PAR.   The Duke knows him for no other but a poor officer of mine;
and writ to me this other day to turn him out o' the band: I think
I have his letter in my pocket.

FIRST SOLD.   Marry, we'll search.

PAR.   In good sadness,[17] I do not know; either it is there, or it is upon
a file with the Duke's other letters in my tent.

FIRST SOLD.   Here 't is; here's a paper: shall I read it to you?

PAR.   I do not know if it be it or no.

BER.   Our interpreter does it well.

FIRST LORD.   Excellently.

FIRST SOLD. [*reads*]   Dian, the count's a fool, and full of gold, —

PAR.   That is not the Duke's letter, sir; that is an advertisement to a
proper maid in Florence, one Diana, to take heed of the allure-
ment of one Count Rousillon, a foolish idle boy, but for all that
very ruttish: I pray you, sir, put it up again.

---

[15]*shrieve's fool*] Here an idiot woman in charge of the sheriff, who was official guardian
of all imbeciles.

[16]*next tile that falls*] a figurative expression for "sudden death."

[17]*in good sadness*] in all seriousness.

FIRST SOLD.   Nay, I'll read it first, by your favour.

PAR.   My meaning in 't, I protest, was very honest in the behalf of the maid; for I knew the young count to be a dangerous and lascivious boy, who is a whale to virginity and devours up all the fry it finds.

BER.   Damnable both-sides rogue!

FIRST SOLD. [*reads*]   When he swears oaths, bid him drop gold, and take it;
> After he scores, he never pays the score:
> Half won is match well made; match, and well make it;
> He ne'er pays after-debts, take it before;
> And say a soldier, Dian, told thee this,
> Men are to mell with, boys are not to kiss:
> For count of this, the count's a fool, I know it,
> Who pays before, but not when he does owe it.

> Thine, as he vowed to thee in thine ear,
> > PAROLLES.

BER.   He shall be whipped through the army with this rhyme in 's forehead.

SEC. LORD.   This is your devoted friend, sir, the manifold linguist and the armipotent soldier.

PAR.   I could endure any thing before but a cat, and now he's a cat to me.

FIRST SOLD.   I perceive, sir, by the general's looks, we shall be fain to hang you.

PAR.   My life, sir, in any case: not that I am afraid to die; but that, my offences being many, I would repent out the remainder of nature: let me live, sir, in a dungeon, i' the stocks, or any where, so I may live.

FIRST SOLD.   We'll see what may be done, so you confess freely; therefore, once more to this Captain Dumain: you have answered to his reputation with the Duke and to his valour: what is his honesty?

PAR.   He will steal, sir, an egg out of a cloister:[18] for rapes and ravishments he parallels Nessus: he professes not keeping of oaths; in breaking 'em he is stronger than Hercules: he will lie, sir, with such volubility, that you would think truth were a fool: drunkenness is his best virtue, for he will be swine-drunk; and in his sleep he does little harm, save to his bed-clothes about him; but they know his conditions and lay him in straw. I have but little more to say, sir, of his honesty: he has every thing that an honest man should not have; what an honest man should have, he has nothing.

---

[18]*steal, sir, an egg . . . cloister*] steal anything, however trifling, from any place however holy. It is possible that "egg" is used here for a young girl.

FIRST LORD.   I begin to love him for this.

BER.   For this description of thine honesty? A pox upon him for me, he's more and more a cat.

FIRST SOLD.   What say you to his expertness in war?

PAR.   Faith, sir, has led the drum before the English tragedians; to belie him, I will not, and more of his soldiership I know not; except, in that country he had the honour to be the officer at a place there called Mile-end,[19] to instruct for the doubling of files: I would do the man what honour I can, but of this I am not certain.

FIRST LORD.   He hath out-villained villany so far, that the rarity redeems him.

BER.   A pox on him, he's a cat still.

FIRST SOLD.   His qualities being at this poor price, I need not to ask you if gold will corrupt him to revolt.

PAR.   Sir, for a quart d'écu he will sell the fee-simple of his salvation, the inheritance of it; and cut the entail from all remainders, and a perpetual succession for it perpetually.[20]

FIRST SOLD.   What's his brother, the other Captain Dumain?

SEC. LORD.   Why does he ask him of me?

FIRST SOLD.   What's he?

PAR.   E'en a crow o' the same nest; not altogether so great as the first in goodness, but greater a great deal in evil: he excels his brother for a coward, yet his brother is reputed one of the best that is: in a retreat he outruns any lackey;[21] marry, in coming on he has the cramp.

FIRST SOLD.   If your life be saved, will you undertake to betray the Florentine?

PAR.   Ay, and the captain of his horse, Count Rousillon.

FIRST SOLD.   I'll whisper with the general, and know his pleasure.

PAR. [*Aside*]   I'll no more drumming; a plague of all drums! Only to seem to deserve well, and to beguile the supposition of that lascivious young boy the count, have I run into this danger. Yet who would have suspected an ambush where I was taken?

FIRST SOLD.   There is no remedy, sir, but you must die: the general says, you that have so traitorously discovered the secrets of your army and made such pestiferous reports of men very nobly held, can serve the world for no honest use; therefore you must die. Come, headsman, off with his head.

PAR.   O Lord, sir, let me live, or let me see my death!

---

[19]*Mile-end*] The drilling ground of the London train bands.

[20]*cut the entail . . . perpetually*] give absolute possession in perpetuity, by freeing the estate of all other claims.

[21]*lackey*] running footman.

FIRST SOLD.   That shall you, and take your leave of all your friends.
                                    [*Unblinding him.*

So, look about you: know you any here?
BER.   Good morrow, noble captain.
SEC. LORD.   God bless you, Captain Parolles.
FIRST LORD.   God save you, noble captain.
SEC. LORD.   Captain, what greeting will you to my Lord Lafeu? I am
    for France.
FIRST LORD.   Good captain, will you give me a copy of the sonnet you
    writ to Diana in behalf of the Count Rousillon? an I were not a
    very coward, I 'ld compel it of you: but fare you well.
                        [*Exeunt* BERTRAM *and* LORDS.
FIRST SOLD.   You are undone, captain, all but your scarf; that has a
    knot on 't yet.
PAR.   Who cannot be crushed with a plot?
FIRST SOLD.   If you could find out a country where but women were
    that had received so much shame, you might begin an impudent
    nation. Fair ye well, sir; I am for France too: we shall speak of you
    there.   [*Exit, with* Soldiers.
PAR.   Yet am I thankful: if my heart were great,
    'T would burst at this. Captain I'll be no more;
    But I will eat and drink, and sleep as soft
    As captain shall: simply the thing I am
    Shall make me live. Who knows himself a braggart,
    Let him fear this, for it will come to pass
    That every braggart shall be found an ass.
    Rust, sword! cool, blushes! and, Parolles, live
    Safest in shame! being fool'd, by foolery thrive!
    There's place and means for every man alive.
    I'll after them.   [*Exit.*

SCENE IV. *Florence: The Widow's House.*

Enter HELENA, Widow, *and* DIANA

HEL.   That you may well perceive I have not wrong'd you,
    One of the greatest in the Christian world
    Shall be my surety; 'fore whose throne 't is needful,
    Ere I can perfect mine intents, to kneel:
    Time was, I did him a desired office,
    Dear almost as his life; which gratitude
    Through flinty Tartar's bosom would peep forth,
    And answer, thanks: I duly am inform'd

His Grace is at Marseilles;[1] to which place
We have convenient convoy. You must know,
I am supposed dead: the army breaking,[2]
My husband hies him home; where, heaven aiding,
And by the leave of my good lord the king,
We'll be before our welcome.

WID.   Gentle madam,
You never had a servant to whose trust
Your business was more welcome.

HEL.   Nor you, mistress,
Ever a friend whose thoughts more truly labour
To recompense your love: doubt not but heaven
Hath brought me up to be your daughter's dower,
As it hath fated her to be my motive[3]
And helper to a husband. But, O strange men!
That can such sweet use make of what they hate,
When saucy trusting of the cozen'd thoughts
Defiles the pitchy night: so lust doth play
With what it loathes for that which is away.
But more of this hereafter. You, Diana,
Under my poor instructions yet must suffer
Something in my behalf.

DIA.   Let death and honesty
Go with your impositions, I am yours
Upon your will to suffer.

HEL.   Yet,[4] I pray you:
But with the word[5] the time will bring on summer,
When briers shall have leaves as well as thorns,
And be as sweet as sharp. We must away;
Our waggon is prepared, and time revives us:
ALL'S WELL THAT ENDS WELL:[6] still the fine 's the crown;
Whate'er the course, the end is the renown.

                                                              [*Exeunt.*

---

[1]*Marseilles*] pronounced as a trisyllable. *Marsellis* is the reading of the Second and
  Third Folios.
[2]*breaking*] disbanding.
[3]*dower . . . motive*] Both words are here used, in conformity with a common
  Elizabethan usage, *viz.*: giver of dower, and supplier of motion, *i.e.* the mover or instrument.
[4]*Yet*] For a while. Cf. 5 lines, *supra*, "yet must suffer."
[5]*with the word*] immediately; as soon as the word is spoken, or promise given.
[6]*All's well that ends well, etc.*] A common proverb. "The fine 's the crown" translates the
  Latin proverb "finis coronat opus."

SCENE V. *Rousillon: The Count's Palace.*

Enter COUNTESS, LAFEU, *and* Clown

LAF. No, no, no, your son was misled with a snipt-taffeta fellow there, whose villanous saffron[1] would have made all the unbaked and doughy youth of a nation in his colour: your daughter-in-law had been alive at this hour, and your son here at home, more advanced by the king than by that red-tailed humble-bee I speak of.

COUNT. I would I had not known him; it was the death of the most virtuous gentlewoman that ever nature had praise for creating. If she had partaken of my flesh, and cost me the dearest groans of a mother, I could not have owed her a more rooted love.

LAF. 'T was a good lady, 't was a good lady: we may pick a thousand salads ere we light on such another herb.

CLO. Indeed, sir, she was the sweet-marjoram of the salad, or rather, the herb of grace.[2]

LAF. They are not herbs, you knave; they are nose-herbs.[3]

CLO. I am no great Nebuchadnezzar, sir; I have not much skill in grass.

LAF. Whether dost thou profess thyself, a knave or a fool?

CLO. A fool, sir, at a woman's service, and a knave at a man's.

LAF. Your distinction?

CLO. I would cozen the man of his wife and do his service.

LAF. So you were a knave at his service, indeed.

CLO. And I would give his wife my bauble, sir, to do her service.

LAF. I will subscribe for thee,[4] thou art both knave and fool.

CLO. At your service.

LAF. No, no, no.

CLO. Why, sir, if I cannot serve you, I can serve as great a prince as you are.

LAF. Who's that? a Frenchman?

CLO. Faith, sir, a' has an English name;[5] but his fisnomy is more hotter in France than there.

LAF. What prince is that?

CLO. The black prince, sir; alias, the prince of darkness; alias, the devil.

---

[1]*saffron*] Saffron was commonly used in the colouring of pastry. Saffron was also a popular dye for both men and women's dress. Reference is here made to both uses of the colouring matter, of which the tinge easily infects its environment.

[2]*herb of grace*] rue.

[3]*nose-herbs*] herbs to be smelled, not eaten.

[4]*I will subscribe for thee*] I'll warrant thee.

[5]*name*] Rowe's satisfactory emendation of the First Folio *maine*.

LAF. Hold thee, there's my purse: I give thee not this to suggest thee
from thy master thou talkest of; serve him still.

CLO. I am a woodland fellow, sir, that always loved a great fire; and
the master I speak of ever keeps a good fire. But, sure, he is the
prince of the world; let his nobility remain in 's court. I am for the
house with the narrow gate, which I take to be too little for pomp
to enter: some that humble themselves may; but the many will be
too chill and tender, and they'll be for the flowery way that leads
to the broad gate and the great fire.

LAF. Go thy ways, I begin to be aweary of thee; and I tell thee so before, because I would not fall out with thee. Go thy ways: let my
horses be well looked to, without any tricks.

CLO. If I put any tricks upon 'em, sir, they shall be jades' tricks;
which are their own right by the law of nature.   [*Exit.*

LAF. A shrewd knave and an unhappy.[6]

COUNT. So he is. My lord that's gone made himself much sport out
of him: by his authority he remains here, which he thinks is a
patent for his sauciness; and, indeed, he has no pace,[7] but runs
where he will.

LAF. I like him well; 't is not amiss. And I was about to tell you, since
I heard of the good lady's death and that my lord your son was
upon his return home, I moved the king my master to speak in the
behalf of my daughter; which, in the minority of them both, his
majesty, out of a self-gracious remembrance, did first propose: his
highness hath promised me to do it: and, to stop up the displeasure he hath conceived against your son, there is no fitter matter.
How does your ladyship like it?

COUNT. With very much content, my lord; and I wish it happily effected.

LAF. His highness comes post from Marseilles, of as able body as
when he numbered thirty: he will be here to-morrow, or I am deceived by him that in such intelligence hath seldom failed.

COUNT. It rejoices me, that I hope I shall see him ere I die. I have letters that my son will be here to-night: I shall beseech your lordship
to remain with me till they meet together.

LAF. Madam, I was thinking with what manners I might safely be ad-
mitted.

COUNT. You need but plead your honourable privilege.

LAF. Lady, of that I have made a bold charter; but I thank my God it
holds yet.

---

[6]A *shrewd knave and an unhappy*] A roguish knave, and one that causes ill-hap or bad
luck.
[7]*he has no pace*] he has no prescribed rule of conduct.

Re-enter Clown

CLO.   O madam, yonder's my lord your son with a patch of velvet on
       's face: whether there be a scar under 't or no, the velvet knows;
       but 't is a goodly patch of velvet: his left cheek is a cheek of two
       pile and a half,[8] but his right cheek is worn bare.
LAF.   A scar nobly got, or a noble scar, is a good livery of honour; so
       belike is that.
CLO.   But it is your carbonadoed face.
LAF.   Let us go see your son, I pray you: I long to talk with the young
       noble soldier.
CLO.   Faith, there's a dozen of 'em, with delicate fine hats and most
       courteous feathers, which bow the head and nod at every man.
                                                                    [*Exeunt*.

[8]*two pile and a half*] a reference to the quality of the velvet of which the patch was
made. Three piled velvet was the best quality.

ACT V.

SCENE I. *Marseilles: A Street.*

Enter HELENA, Widow, *and* DIANA, *with two* Attendants

HELENA.　But this exceeding posting day and night.
　　Must wear your spirits low; we cannot help it:
　　But since you have made the days and nights as one,
　　To wear your gentle limbs in my affairs,
　　Be bold you do so grow in my requital
　　As nothing can unroot you.[1] In happy time;

Enter a Gentleman[2]

　　This man may help me to his majesty's ear,
　　If he would spend his power. God save you, sir.
GENT.　And you.
HEL.　Sir, I have seen you in the court of France.
GENT.　I have been sometimes there.
HEL.　I do presume, sir, that you are not fallen
　　From the report that goes upon your goodness;
　　And therefore, goaded with most sharp occasions,[3]
　　Which lay nice manners by, I put you to
　　The use of your own virtues, for the which
　　I shall continue thankful.
GENT.　　　　　　　　　What's your will?
HEL.　That it will please you
　　To give this poor petition to the king,
　　And aid me with that store of power you have
　　To come into his presence.

---

[1]*Be bold . . . unroot you*] Be assured that the claims on my recognition are growing so great that nothing can cancel them.
[2]*Enter a Gentleman*] This is Rowe's emendation of the First Folio reading, *Enter a gentle Astringer* (*i.e.* falconer), a reading which the text fails to justify.
[3]*goaded . . . occasions*] incited by most pressing needs.

73

GENT.   The king's not here.

HEL.   Not here, sir!

GENT.   Not, indeed:
He hence removed last night and with more haste
Than is his use.

WID.   Lord, how we lose our pains!

HEL.   ALL'S WELL THAT ENDS WELL yet,
Though time seem so adverse and means unfit.
I do beseech you, whither is he gone?

GENT.   Marry, as I take it, to Rousillon;
Whither I am going.

HEL.   I do beseech you, sir,
Since you are like to see the king before me,
Commend the paper to his gracious hand,
Which I presume shall render you no blame
But rather make you thank your pains for it.
I will come after you with what good speed
Our means will make us means.

GENT.   This I'll do for you.

HEL.   And you shall find yourself to be well thank'd,
Whate'er falls more. We must to horse again.
Go, go, provide.

                                                    [*Exeunt.*

SCENE II. *Rousillon: Before the Count's Palace.*

Enter Clown, *and* PAROLLES, *following*

PAR.   Good Monsieur Lavache, give my Lord Lafeu this letter: I
have ere now, sir, been better known to you, when I have held
familiarity with fresher clothes; but I am now, sir, muddied in
fortune's mood, and smell somewhat strong of her strong displeasure.

CLO.   Truly, fortune's displeasure is but sluttish, if it smell so strongly
as thou speakest of: I will henceforth eat no fish of fortune's but-
tering. Prithee, allow the wind.

PAR.   Nay, you need not to stop your nose, sir; I spake but by a
metaphor.

CLO.   Indeed, sir, if your metaphor stink, I will stop my nose; or
against any man's metaphor. Prithee, get thee further.

PAR.   Pray you, sir, deliver me this paper.

CLO.   Foh! prithee, stand away: a paper from fortune's close-stool to give to a nobleman! Look, here he comes himself.

Enter LAFEU

Here is a purr of fortune's, sir, or of fortune's cat,[1]—but not a musk-cat,—that has fallen into the unclean fishpond of her displeasure, and, as he says, is muddied withal: pray you, sir, use the carp as you may; for he looks like a poor, decayed, ingenious, foolish, rascally knave. I do pity his distress in my similes[2] of comfort and leave him to your lordship.

[*Exit.*

PAR.   My lord, I am a man whom fortune hath cruelly scratched.

LAF.   And what would you have me to do? 'T is too late to pare her nails now. Wherein have you played the knave with fortune, that she should scratch you, who of herself is a good lady and would not have knaves thrive long under her? There's a quart d'écu for you: let the justices make you and fortune friends: I am for other business.

PAR.   I beseech your honour to hear me one single word.

LAF.   You beg a single penny more: come, you shall ha 't; save your word.

PAR.   My name, my good lord, is Parolles.

LAF.   You beg more than "word,"[3] then. Cox my passion! give me your hand. How does your drum?

PAR.   O my good lord, you were the first that found me!

LAF.   Was I, in sooth? and I was the first that lost thee.

PAR.   It lies in you, my lord, to bring me in some grace, for you did bring me out.

LAF.   Out upon thee, knave! dost thou put upon me at once both the office of God and the devil? One brings thee in grace and the other brings thee out. [*Trumpets sound.*] The king's coming; I know by his trumpets. Sirrah, inquire further after me; I had talk of you last night: though you are a fool and a knave, you shall eat; go to, follow.

PAR.   I praise God for you.

[*Exeunt.*

---

[1] *purr of fortune's . . . cat*] Parolles' speech is contemptuously compared to the murmurings of a cat.
[2] *similes*] Theobald's emendation of the First Folio reading *smiles*.
[3] *more than "word"*] an obvious quibble on the fact that "Parolles" (*i.e.* paroles) is the plural of the French *parole* (*i.e.* word).

SCENE III. *Rousillon: The Count's Palace.*

Flourish. Enter KING, COUNTESS, LAFEU, *the two* French Lords, *with* Attendants

KING.   We lost a jewel of her; and our esteem[1]
Was made much poorer by it: but your son,
As mad in folly, lack'd the sense to know
Her estimation home.[2]

COUNT.   'T is past, my liege;
And I beseech your majesty to make it
Natural rebellion, done i' the blaze[3] of youth;
When oil and fire, too strong for reason's force,
O'erbears it and burns on.

KING.   My honour'd lady,
I have forgiven and forgotten all;
Though my revenges were high bent upon him,
And watch'd the time to shoot.

LAF.   This I must say,
But first I beg my pardon, the young lord
Did to his majesty, his mother and his lady
Offence of mighty note; but to himself
The greatest wrong of all. He lost a wife
Whose beauty did astonish the survey
Of richest eyes,[4] whose words all ears took captive,
Whose dear perfection hearts that scorn'd to serve
Humbly call'd mistress.

KING.   Praising what is lost
Makes the remembrance dear. Well, call him hither;
We are reconciled, and the first view shall kill
All repetition: let him not ask our pardon;
The nature of his great offence is dead,
And deeper than oblivion we do bury
The incensing relics[5] of it: let him approach,
A stranger, no offender; and inform him
So 't is our will he should.

GENT.   I shall, my liege.
                                             [*Exit.*

KING.   What says he to your daughter? have you spoke?

---

[1]*our esteem*] the esteem in which we held the world at large, or things in general.
[2]*know . . . home*] thoroughly appreciate her worth.
[3]*blaze*] Theobald's emendation of the reading of the Folios, *blade*.
[4]*richest eyes*] eyes that have seen most beauty.
[5]*incensing relics*] surviving details capable of incensing us.

LAF.   All that he is hath reference to your highness.[6]
KING.   Then shall we have a match. I have letters sent me
  That set him high in fame.

Enter BERTRAM

LAF.   He looks well on 't.
KING.   I am not a day of season,[7]
  For thou mayst see a sunshine and a hail
  In me at once: but to the brightest beams
  Distracted clouds give way; so stand thou forth;
  The time is fair again.
BER.   My high-repented blames,
  Dear sovereign, pardon to me.
KING.   All is whole;
  Not one word more of the consumed time.
  Let's take the instant by the forward top;
  For we are old, and on our quick'st decrees
  The inaudible and noiseless foot of Time
  Steals ere we can effect them. You remember
  The daughter of this lord?
BER.   Admiringly, my liege, at first
  I stuck my choice upon her, ere my heart
  Durst make too bold a herald of my tongue:
  Where the impression of mine eye infixing,
  Contempt his scornful perspective[8] did lend me,
  Which warp'd the line of every other favour;
  Scorn'd a fair colour, or express'd it stolen;
  Extended or contracted all proportions
  To a most hideous object: thence it came
  That she whom all men praised and whom myself,
  Since I have lost, have loved, was in mine eye
  The dust that did offend it.
KING.   Well excused:
  That thou didst love her, strikes some scores away
  From the great compt: but love that comes too late,
  Like a remorseful pardon slowly carried,
  To the great sender turns a sour offence,
  Crying "That's good that's gone." Our rash faults
  Make trivial price of serious things we have,
  Not knowing them until we know their grave:

[6]*All . . . highness*] He refers himself entirely, wholly submits to your highness.
[7]*a day of season*] a seasonable day, in which the weather is all of the same character.
[8]*perspective*] a glass or sort of telescope that distorts the object to which it is directed.

Oft our displeasures, to ourselves unjust,
Destroy our friends and after weep their dust:
Our own love waking cries to see what's done,
While shameful hate sleeps out the afternoon.[9]
Be this sweet Helen's knell, and now forget her.
Send forth your amorous token for fair Maudlin:
The main consents are had; and here we'll stay
To see our widower's second marriage-day.

COUNT.   Which better than the first, O dear heaven, bless!
Or ere they meet, in me, O nature, cesse![10]

LAF.   Come on, my son, in whom my house's name
Must be digested,[11] give a favour from you
To sparkle in the spirits of my daughter,
That she may quickly come. [BERTRAM *gives a ring*.] By my old
      beard,
And every hair that's on 't, Helen, that's dead,
Was a sweet creature: such a ring as this,
The last[12] that e'er I took her leave at court,
I saw upon her finger.

BER.   Hers it was not.

KING.   Now, pray you, let me see it; for mine eye,
While I was speaking, oft was fasten'd to 't.
This ring was mine; and, when I gave it Helen,
I bade her, if her fortunes ever stood
Necessitied to help, that by this token
I would relieve her. Had you that craft, to reave her
Of what should stead her most?

BER.   My gracious sovereign,
Howe'er it pleases you to take it so,
The ring was never hers.

COUNT.   Son, on my life,
I have seen her wear it; and she reckon'd it
At her life's rate.

LAF.   I am sure I saw her wear it.

BER.   You are deceived, my lord; she never saw it:
In Florence was it from a casement thrown me,
Wrapp'd in a paper, which contain'd the name

---

[9]*While . . . afternoon*] On the other hand, downright shameful hate (incapable of love's
remorse) goes on enjoying its habitual afternoon slumbers unconcerned by any havoc
that it may have worked.
[10]*cesse*] the old spelling of "cease," retained here for the sake of the rhyme.
[11]*digested*] incorporated.
[12]*The last*] The last time.

Of her that threw it: noble she was, and thought
I stood engaged: but when I had subscribed
To mine own fortune[13] and inform'd her fully
I could not answer in that course of honour
As she had made the overture, she ceased
In heavy satisfaction[14] and would never
Receive the ring again.

KING.   Plutus himself,
That knows the tinct and multiplying medicine,[15]
Hath not in nature's mystery more science
Than I have in this ring: 't was mine, 't was Helen's,
Whoever gave it you. Then, if you know
That you are well acquainted with yourself,
Confess 't was hers, and by what rough enforcement
You got it from her: she call'd the saints to surety
That she would never put it from her finger,
Unless she gave it to yourself in bed,
Where you have never come, or sent it us
Upon her great disaster.

BER.   She never saw it.

KING.   Thou speak'st it falsely, as I love mine honour;
And makest conjectural fears to come into me,
Which I would fain shut out. If it should prove
That thou art so inhuman, — 't will not prove so; —
And yet I know not: thou didst hate her deadly,
And she is dead; which nothing, but to close
Her eyes myself, could win me to believe,
More than to see this ring. Take him away.

                            [Guards seize BERTRAM.
My fore-past proofs, howe'er the matter fall,
Shall tax my fears of little[16] vanity,
Having vainly fear'd too little. Away with him!
We'll sift this matter further.

BER.   If you shall prove
This ring was ever hers, you shall as easy

---

[13]*I stood engaged . . . fortune*] I stood engaged to her; but when I had formally given my consent to what my fortune required.

[14]*In heavy satisfaction*] Sorrowfully admitting that she was satisfied (of my obligation elsewhere).

[15]*tinct and multiplying medicine*] the alchemical tincture or elixir which multiplies gold by transmuting into it other metals.

[16]*My fore-past proofs . . . little*] However the matter turn out, the proofs I have already got together are sufficient to relieve my fears of any suspicion of their being vain or groundless. Hitherto I have ineptly been too little suspicious.

Prove that I husbanded her bed in Florence,
Where yet she never was. [*Exit, guarded.*
KING. I am wrapp'd in dismal thinkings.

Enter a Gentleman

GENT. Gracious sovereign,
Whether I have been to blame or no, I know not:
Here's a petition from a Florentine,
Who hath for four or five removes come short
To tender it herself. I undertook it,
Vanquish'd thereto by the fair grace and speech
Of the poor suppliant, who by this I know
Is here attending: her business looks in her
With an importing visage; and she told me,
In a sweet verbal brief,[17] it did concern
Your highness with herself.

KING. [*reads*] Upon his many protestations to marry me when his wife was dead, I blush to say it, he won me. Now is the Count Rousillon a widower: his vows are forfeited to me, and my honour's paid to him. He stole from Florence, taking no leave, and I follow him to his country for justice: grant it me, O king! in you it best lies; otherwise a seducer flourishes, and a poor maid is undone.

DIANA CAPILET.

LAF. I will buy me a son-in-law in a fair, and toll[18] for this: I'll none of him.

KING. The heavens have thought well on thee, Lafeu,
To bring forth this discovery. Seek these suitors:
Go speedily and bring again the count.
I am afeard the life of Helen, lady,
Was foully snatch'd.

COUNT. Now, justice on the doers!

Re-enter BERTRAM, *guarded*

KING. I wonder, sir, sith wives are monsters to you,
And that you fly them as you swear them lordship,[19]
Yet you desire to marry.

Enter Widow *and* DIANA

What woman's that?

---

[17]*a sweet verbal brief*] Cf. note 15, page 30, "the now-born *brief*."
[18]*toll*] pay toll for him, like the purchaser of a horse at a fair; come honestly by him.
[19]*swear them lordship*] swear (in the marriage service) to become their lords.

DIA.   I am, my lord, a wretched Florentine,
      Derived from the ancient Capilet:
      My suit, as I do understand, you know,
      And therefore know how far I may be pitied.
WID.   I am her mother, sir, whose age and honour
      Both suffer under this complaint we bring,
      And both shall cease, without your remedy.[20]
KING.   Come hither, count; do you know these women?
BER.   My lord, I neither can nor will deny
      But that I know them: do they charge me further?
DIA.   Why do you look so strange upon your wife?
BER.   She's none of mine, my lord.
DIA.   If you shall marry,
      You give away this hand, and that is mine;
      You give away heaven's vows, and those are mine;
      You give away myself, which is known mine;
      For I by vow am so embodied yours,
      That she which marries you must marry me,
      Either both or none.
LAF.   Your reputation comes too short for my daughter; you are no
      husband for her.
BER.   My lord, this is a fond and desperate creature,
      Whom sometime I have laugh'd with: let your highness
      Lay a more noble thought upon mine honour
      Than for to think that I would sink it here.
KING.   Sir, for my thoughts, you have them ill to friend
      Till your deeds gain them: fairer prove your honour
      Than in my thought it lies.
DIA.   Good my lord,
      Ask him upon his oath, if he does think
      He had not my virginity.
KING.   What say'st thou to her?
BER.   She's impudent, my lord,
      And was a common gamester to the camp.
DIA.   He does me wrong, my lord; if I were so,
      He might have bought me at a common price:
      Do not believe him. O, behold this ring,
      Whose high respect and rich validity
      Did lack a parallel; yet for all that
      He gave it to a commoner o' the camp,
      If I be one.

---

[20]*both . . . remedy*] both shall perish, unless you give the remedy.

COUNT.   He blushes, and 't is it:
   Of six preceding ancestors, that gem,
   Conferr'd by testament to the sequent issue,
   Hath it been owed and worn. This is his wife;
   That ring's a thousand proofs.
KING.   Methought you said
   You saw one here in court could witness it.
DIA.   I did, my lord, but loath am to produce
   So bad an instrument: his name's Parolles.
LAF.   I saw the man to-day, if man he be.
KING.   Find him, and bring him hither.

                                 [*Exit an Attendant.*
BER.   What of him?
   He's quoted for a most perfidious slave,
   With all the spots o' the world tax'd and debosh'd;
   Whose nature sickens but to speak a truth.
   Am I or that or this for what he'll utter,
   That will speak any thing?
KING.   She hath that ring of yours.
BER.   I think she has: certain it is I liked her,
   And boarded her i' the wanton way of youth:
   She knew her distance, and did angle for me,
   Madding my eagerness with her restraint,
   As all impediments in fancy's course
   Are motives of more fancy;[21] and, in fine,
   Her infinite cunning,[22] with her modern grace,
   Subdued me to her rate:[23] she got the ring;
   And I had that which any inferior might
   At market-price have bought.
DIA.   I must be patient:
   You, that have turn'd off a first so noble wife,
   May justly diet me.[24] I pray you yet,
   Since you lack virtue I will lose a husband,

---

[21]*As all impediments . . . fancy*] As all obstructions in the way of love only incite its increase.

[22]*Her infinite cunning*] The First Folio reading is *Her insuite comming*, of which no sense has been made. The felicitous emendation in the text is due to Sidney Walker. "Modern grace" may be "modish grace." But the conjectural reading, *modest grace*, deserves attention.

[23]*Subdued me to her rate*] Brought me to accept her terms.

[24]*diet me*] Perhaps this may mean "prescribe for me a regimen or course of living." Cf. note 6 on page 60. The reading is generally held to be corrupt. The meaning required seems to be something like "feed on me."

Send for your ring, I will return it home,
And give me mine again.

BER.   I have it not.

KING.   What ring was yours, I pray you?

DIA.   Sir, much like
The same upon your finger.

KING.   Know you this ring? this ring was his of late.

DIA.   And this was it I gave him, being abed.

KING.   The story then goes false, you threw it him
Out of a casement.

DIA.   I have spoke the truth.

Enter PAROLLES

BER.   My lord, I do confess the ring was hers.

KING.   You boggle shrewdly, every feather starts you.
Is this the man you speak of?

DIA.   Ay, my lord.

KING.   Tell me, sirrah, but tell me true, I charge you,
Not fearing the displeasure of your master,
Which on your just proceeding I'll keep off,
By him and by this woman here what know you?

PAR.   So please your majesty, my master hath been an honourable
gentleman: tricks he hath had in him, which gentlemen have.

KING.   Come, come, to the purpose: did he love this woman?

PAR.   Faith, sir, he did love her; but how?

KING.   How, I pray you?

PAR.   He did love her, sir, as a gentleman loves a woman.

KING.   How is that?

PAR.   He loved her, sir, and loved her not.

KING.   As thou art a knave, and no knave. What an equivocal companion is this!

PAR.   I am a poor man, and at your majesty's command.

LAF.   He's a good drum, my lord, but a naughty orator.

DIA.   Do you know he promised me marriage?

PAR.   Faith, I know more than I'll speak.

KING.   But wilt thou not speak all thou knowest?

PAR.   Yes, so please your majesty. I did go between them, as I said; but more
than that, he loved her: for indeed he was mad for her, and talked of
Satan, and of Limbo, and of Furies, and I know not what: yet I was in
that credit with them at that time, that I knew of their going to bed, and
of other motions, as promising her marriage, and things which would
derive me ill will[25] to speak of; therefore I will not speak what I know.

---

[25]*derive me ill will*] get me, bring down on me, ill will.

KING. Thou hast spoken all already, unless thou canst say they are
married: but thou art too fine[26] in thy evidence; therefore stand
aside.
This ring, you say, was yours?
DIA. Ay, my good lord.
KING. Where did you buy it? or who gave it you?
DIA. It was not given me, nor I did not buy it.
KING. Who lent it you?
DIA. It was not lent me neither.
KING. Where did you find it, then?
DIA. I found it not.
KING. If it were yours by none of all these ways,
How could you give it him?
DIA. I never gave it him.
LAF. This woman's an easy glove, my lord; she goes off and on at
pleasure.
KING. This ring was mine; I gave it his first wife.
DIA. It might be yours or hers, for aught I know.
KING. Take her away; I do not like her now;
To prison with her: and away with him.
Unless thou tell'st me where thou hadst this ring,
Thou diest within this hour.
DIA. I'll never tell you.
KING. Take her away.
DIA. I'll put in bail, my liege.
KING. I think thee now some common customer.
DIA. By Jove, if ever I knew man, 't was you.
KING. Wherefore hast thou accused him all this while?
DIA. Because he's guilty, and he is not guilty:
He knows I am no maid, and he'll swear to 't;
I'll swear I am a maid, and he knows not.
Great king, I am no strumpet, by my life;
I am either maid, or else this old man's wife.
KING. She does abuse our ears: to prison with her.
DIA. Good mother, fetch my bail. Stay, royal sir:

[*Exit* Widow.

The jeweller that owes the ring is sent for,
And he shall surety me. But for this lord,
Who hath abused me, as he knows himself,
Though yet he never harm'd me, here I quit him:
He knows himself my bed he hath defiled;
And at that time he got his wife with child:

[26]*too fine*] too subtle, artful.

Dead though she be, she feels her young one kick:
So there's my riddle,—One that's dead is quick:
And now behold the meaning.

Re-enter Widow, *with* HELENA

KING.   Is there no exorcist²⁷
Beguiles the truer office of mine eyes?
Is 't real that I see?
HEL.   No, my good lord;
'T is but the shadow of a wife you see,
The name and not the thing.
BER.   Both, both. O, pardon!
HEL.   O my good lord, when I was like this maid,
I found you wondrous kind. There is your ring;
And, look you, here's your letter; this it says:
"When from my finger you can get this ring
And are by me with child," &c. This is done:
Will you be mine, now you are doubly won?
BER.   If she, my liege, can make me know this clearly,
I'll love her dearly, ever, ever dearly.
HEL.   If it appear not plain and prove untrue,
Deadly divorce step between me and you!
O my dear mother, do I see you living?
LAF.   Mine eyes smell onions; I shall weep anon: [*To* PAROLLES] Good
Tom Drum, lend me a handkercher: so, I thank thee: wait on me
home, I'll make sport with thee: let thy courtesies alone, they are
scurvy ones.
KING.   Let us from point to point this story know,
To make the even truth in pleasure flow.
[*To* DIANA] If thou be'st yet a fresh uncropped flower,
Choose thou thy husband, and I'll pay thy dower;
For I can guess that by thy honest aid
. Thou kept'st a wife herself, thyself a maid.
Of that and all the progress, more and less,
Resolvedly more leisure shall express:
All yet seems well; and if it end so meet,
The bitter past, more welcome is the sweet.

                                          [*Flourish.*

---

²⁷*exorcist*] one who raises spirits.

EPILOGUE

KING.   The king's a beggar, now the play is done:
    All is well ended, if this suit be won,
    That you express content; which we will pay,
    With strife to please you, day exceeding day:
    Ours be your patience then, and yours our parts;[1]
    Your gentle hands lend us, and take our hearts.

                                              [Exeunt.

[1]*parts*] abilities.